THE ARVINSTRUM
Book 3

THE NIVIAN KING SERIES BOOKS

The Nivian King: Book 1
The Ice Scabbard: Book 2
The Arvinstrum: Book 3
The Army of Naquior: Book 4

SELECT NONFICTION

Persons Artificial
The Earth-Colonizing Handbook of Generation Stelan
God is DNA
The Science of Reality
Grand Robot
World War C

THE ARVINSTRUM
Book 3

PARIS TOSEN

Tosen Books

The Arvinstrum: Book 3 is a work of fiction.

ISBN: 978-1-926949-22-2

www.tosen.ca

Book design and cover by Paris Tosen

THE ARVINSTRUM

Only knowledge is infinite.

— Kozotalian proverb

Chapter 1

CALWIN AND Ralwindale were luxuriously dressed at *Yapallonia*, a ritzy members-only club, enjoying the night with the other rich portion of the ceramination. Sparse member clubs had sprouted in response to the economic rise in Casus and were chosen locations for the wealthy who wanted to make their distinctions known. After an entire evening of superficial talk and an excessive intake of wanine, the couple exited the front doors and, in giggly fashion, crossed the empty street.

A lone cloaked figure watched from the shadows, refusing to take the eyes off of the two until they had gone far down the street. At that point the stranger trailed a safe distance until they reached a twin set of towers and both entered inside.

The dark figure stood staring silently for half-an-hour and then, quick as a flamma bolt, ran off into the darkness. It scaled – floating along the walls height rather than pulling – two walls avoiding a guard unit then found the back of a run-down building, leapt up and caught the open window on the third floor without a sound. One flip and it was gone. Moving less cautiously it drew back the hood on the cloak and walked over to a half-lit room.

"We're you followed?" a voice in the dark asked.

"No. Nothing is out there."

"Did you find them?"

"Yeah, I found one."

"Who?"

"Calwin," said Khan, stepping into the lit area to reveal his face. Shev'la Khan did not know whether to be angry or sad after what he had just witnessed. Since they had re-entered Casus, they were warned by Mok of Gurney's crew that the Seronian Guard wanted their heads. It had more to do with the death of Captain T. Rain than anything else but rumors spread that Thryn had his hand in the deal in case his old partner survived.

"Was she with that mud-cerbi?"

"She was with another," said Khan, not knowing how to tell Griz about Ralwindale but then just decided to come out with it. "The other is Ralwindale, a wealthy ventan, he gave me the locator device, but…"

"What is wrong, Khan?"

"…the Ralwindale I met before and the one I saw tonight is not the same."

"A mistake?"

"I don't know. I overheard her mention his name twice.—That slut. It sure was him, but if that was him who did I meet before?"

Khan withdrew the locator device he picked up on the way out of the tomb – happily discarded by his ex-lutafriend – held it up, then something strange occurred. The device lit up white all around.

"What's going on?" he said as his body reacted in surprise.

"Wasn't that device for the tomb?" said Griz.

"Yes…maybe…no," the young wind master started and stopped as a glimmer flashed in his eyes. "It wasn't for the tomb." He felt for his purple sack, placing Pyxacognitartis on a small table. The locator device continued to glow brightly. "It wasn't meant to locate the tomb. It was meant to locate this cylindrical case. And if that wasn't Ralwindale, then the imposter wanted this thing for an important reason or he wouldn't have constructed such a mathematical medium."

"How did you meet this luto? Was he a friend of yours?"

"It was all very strange. It happened in the tavern. We started talking and he said some things about my father and then sooner than you know it he told me to go to the Inist islands. He gave me this device, no questions asked."

"If he wanted you to get it, maybe he wants it for himself. Did you think of that?"

"Not until now. But why me?" Khan asked, perplexed. "And if he wanted it, why hasn't he come to get it?"

"You are asking me this question?"

"Why find me and entrust this in my hands?" Khan now felt Pyxacognitartis, feeling the engravings with his bare fingers. "Something is inside of you, Pyxa. Something is there."

"Khan, we have to kill Thryn."

"I know," said Khan, getting back to the topic at hand and not the one preferred. "Soon enough he will find Calwin and when he does we will be there for him. Tomorrow, I will get a tard and see if we can't track him that way. And, better yet, I will get rid of this locator device. If it can find the device it can also find us."

Griz mostly stayed out of sight for the next day and chose to practice with his battle clavus enjoying his new found strength.

It was much too dangerous to be exposed after they were marked for killing Captain T. Rain, but his patience was wearing thin. Khan could sneak around much more easily and tracked Calwin's movements. He let a thief steal the locator from him in the afternoon. It reminded him of the escapade with Boon and when he lost his father's manuscripts. He laughed at the stupidity of thieves and how they fail to consider the consequences of their actions. Experience was a qualified teacher and the thief would learn that.

CALWIN SPENT a lot of time at Yapallonia with different lutos, probably high officials. On the third straight night at the club he was there with her. A call came in, perfect timing, and Khan was ready to trace the direction of the photon rays. He caught a glimpse of the image Thryn spoke to and it raised his left eyebrow. Hirimo's face was there. The assassin was still around after all.

Once locked on, he waited until Thryn and Calwin were a good distance away then made his call. Thryn answered anonymously. Khan kept his hood up and back turned.

"Life is good for you these days," said Khan.

"Who is this? Show your face," said Thryn.

"Always taking care of yourself, I see."

"It is a familiar voice, one who seems to have risen from the dead."

Khan removed his hood. "I have risen to claim the shares owed."

"The shares have been spent—"

"Do not play your game with me, Thryn. Do not play me as you have played Calwin."

"I will send you to your tomb for this—"

"Shut up. Prepare the share of wealth owed by tomorrow night. That's tomorrow night. And don't forget what's owed to Griz." With that, the image and signal died out.

"That morbfarcking Serag penis! He lives. This will have to change," Thryn said.

"What are you going to do?" she asked.

"I'll show him that chasing me is more deadly than any tomb he might encounter." Thryn connected with Hirimo's tard. "It's me."

"Speak."

"The two of them are here. You have been paid the first half and will get the other half when it is done. I want it done by the morning. Is that clear?"

"By morning, the street will be clean but you'll have to add twenty percent."

"Fine. But have it done."

Once the final part of the conversation was overheard, Khan crawled away into the night and returned to his temporary residence. Griz had already hacked and thrashed much of the half-empty warehouse so it didn't look much different except for the gouge of a clavus blade here and there.

"Our play is in motion," said Khan. "Hirimo is on us. I am sure that the assassin will track the tard here as I am sure that the assassin will find his own tomb in this broken down place. First the assassin then—"

"Thryn."

"There were never so many assassins and thieves when I was younger. They grow with zorn and I can only predict an increase in their vile numbers. Wealth attracts the undesirables."

"Fortunate that Hirimo will not receive a statue for his murders," said Griz.

Khan moved about making preparations for the assassin's arrival. It did not make him feel welcome to have so many after him and his friend. The thought bothered him more when he remembered that it was he who had led the mission to Escarotion's Tomb and it was he who – after barely surviving – was left empty handed and poor as before, in fact, poorer. He knew that adventures were made possible because of risk but did not realize the value of quality party members, if that characteristic could be measured.

Griz, from Khan's perspective, was becoming more eager to kill than before. When he had first met the lug, Griz resolved disputes with his fists or weapons that usually ended in a milky floor. But Griz actually desired to kill rather than killing as a result of a situation that upset him.

Khan had to watch this more closely to see if those changes were indeed real. What if it had to do with being in Escoration's cerbind and brought up some repressed memories of his father? What if there was something happening to me? thought Khan. All he could do was to keep himself busy and be watchful.

He had one certainty and that was his life was about to evolve, and it was about time. He was tiring of these silly adventures only for the glory of zorn. There was no glory in zorn. There was no feeling to earning zorn and earning it made him feel even more empty.

Khan shared some similarities with his father. His father was curious about things, and because life on Seranor offered so many things of curiosity, his father was always intrigued and happy by its abundance. Khan felt some of that growing in him. The need to explore for learning sake rather than for zorn sake. Perhaps, he thought, Pyxa was given to him for that very reason of exploration and in its exploration he could continue to evolve.

THE TARD was placed on the second floor at the top of the staircase where it was in the open. Two sacks of mud covered by Khan's cloak was put by the tard simulating a body. The nearest window was in a room far over to the right with the door shut tight. Along the second floor hallway was placed broken glass over a length too long to jump. This left only two access points exposed – the skylight and the stairs. Two was preferred over one as it made the set up less obvious.

Khan waited on the second floor behind the railing and two meters from the door to the room. Griz, because of his bulky body, waited downstairs with his clavus. He had removed his armor, reluctantly, in order to be more silent.

Assassins were good at two things, killing and sensing traps. Khan hoped that the surprise factor under pressured conditions would be enough to catch him slightly off guard. In hand-to-hand combat Hirimo couldn't beat the two of them head on and once inside that would be the only way out.

Later in the night, a sound awoke Khan's light sleep, the creaky skylight opened. A barely visible rope was lowered and a body along with it. Griz was ready downstairs. The assassin moved cautiously and with a sense of precision in his trade. He dropped the last meter, looked around with its hood up, then approached the sacks of mud disguised as sleeping entans.

At that moment, Griz accidentally brushed his clavus blade against the wall and the assassin moved backwards toward the staircase slowly unsheathing his batier. Back and further back he walked making his way down the dirty stairs.

Thinking that they would lose their chance, Khan leaped over the rail withdrawing a batier all in one motion and landing six steps above the cloaked figure.

"Time to die, Hirimo," said Khan.

The assassin ran down the stairs trying to avoid combat but Griz was there to prevent his escape. Khan closed in with full bore and the two battled. His wind movements proved useful on the stairs and he gained the upper hand while Griz guarded the escape route.

Just when he thought the play had gone well, Khan caught a shadow behind his hulky friend and gave a short warning, just enough for him to shift his body. Had he remained in his position, Griz would have died instantly; instead, the batier pierced a non-vital organ and the angered hulk chased after his own aggressor.

The undeterred warrior faced his opponent, Hirimo, once more. Khan's battle did not last and his batier pierced deeply several times downing his enemy in dripping milk. Under the hood was another face, a twin like Hirimo but not Hirimo.

By the time Khan reached his friend, the real Hirimo was dead. Griz's ability in hand-to-hand far outmatched the skill of an assassin and Hirimo was left in three large pieces.

"Thanks," said Griz.

"You just can't stop hacking body parts, can you?" said Khan.

"It's just the way I fight."

"It's a milkbath that leaves a farcking big mess."

"Thryn must die or it will never finish."

"What is it with thieves, anyway? They just have their own greedy ideas. Remind me not to have any more thieves in our party," added Khan to make his point.

Chapter 2

NIGHT BECAME a bright day as Seranor once again woke the inhabitants of the planet. Seronians stirred early in the streets enjoying the goodness of the morning, as well as the peace that came with it. More and more entans clambered out of their comfortable beds and soon the streets were filled with the vibrancy of an urba.

Khan and Griz walked among them, slightly disguised to prevent easy recognition. They walked straight to a higher-classed inn and entered the dining room where a handful had come to have breakfast. The table was loaded with steamy dishes of clay; all colors and shapes and consistencies. Its smell even slowed down Khan enough to inhale more deeply.

The two of them, armed with a sheathed batier and a concealed battle clavus, walked in quietly though in a half-crazed state. In his left hand, Khan carried a small bag that swished an object inside, ever so gently, as he walked.

Thryn was there with Calwin. They had just ordered their food and were about to sit down to a clay breakfast when the interruption came.

"You two are so predictable—Where's our share?" said Khan, nonchalantly.

"You're back. Congratulations. Look what loyalty did to you this time," said Thryn as he caressed Calwin's hips.

"Are you finished, Thief?"

"Your optimism impresses me, Khan. I'm sure that is what impressed Calwin, but optimism is empty without well-planned execution."

"Optimism brought me here, did it not?"

"Optimism is oxy with nothing to consume except what happens to be around. It is dangerous."

"This is not a discussion, Thief.—Here, this is for you." Khan tossed the little bag at him.

"What is this?"

"Open it and see," said Khan.

Thryn opened the bag enough to see a milky hand inside with Hirimo's familiar ring on the second finger. Calwin lost her appetite that very second.

"That is right, it is dangerous, Thief."

"Me, a thief? What are you, are you not a thief?" He dropped the bag on the table.

"Not like you. You stole my luta with your lies and made her into a thief like you. The worst kind of thief," said Khan. "But she is smart now, isn't that right, Calwin." He smiled at her showing that he knew something about what she had been doing with the other officials.

"Khan, why do you always bring trouble?" she said.

"Calwin came willingly. Careers have charisma. Your problem is that you care too much and try to hard," said Thryn.

"I didn't care about the damn wench neither do I care about you. Stop talking and start paying," Khan said as he unsheathed his batier and pointed it at his enemy.

Griz waited for the first action. The hunger pain stiffened his body.

"Calwin, tell him," said Thryn.

"What now?" she said.

"Calwin!" he repeated.

"Who wants to talk with you?" she said. Seeing Khan alive brought back her feelings for him and she could not deny those feelings of love.

Two well-dressed security guards came over. They were armed with single-handed clavuses. Griz smirked at their tiny weapons and raised his own.

"Take out my friends, will you," said Thryn.

"Where is our share? That's all we want," said Khan. Griz didn't agree with that.

The two trained lutos moved up close.

"Guards," said Thryn, "take these morb to their rightful place."

"Wait. Before we complicate things let's..." The guards motioned to grab Khan but his fast reactions surprised them both. A heavy battle clavus hacked off both outstretched arms of one of the guards above the elbow. He ran screaming in pain and spraying his milk all over the room. For the other, Khan locked his joints and dislocated both his arms then tripped him onto the table breaking his face and putting him out. Panic hit the breakfast patrons and leisurely dressed Seronians, unfamiliar with battle, dashed about like wild snakes. A few remained calm and bored by such seedishness. Thryn was ready to fight by then and may have been his plan all along.

"Please, Thryn," said Calwin.

"All right. Wait here," said the Thief.

"No, we're going together," said Khan.

"Fine. It's upstairs," he replied.

The foursome soon reached a lavish cell and Thryn took out a large box filled with odd objects.

Griz held Calwin. She could not escape his grasp nor was allowed to cast a spell.

"Dump it on the bed," Khan said.

He did so and many items fell out but none of what was their treasure or a tard that might have contained zorn.

KHAN RUMAGED through the junk. It laughed at him and his disappointments. How long can a fool play the fool? He finally grabbed the entire box and threw it to the wall yelling out loudly.

Thryn took his initiative and attacked Khan with a short batier hidden behind a table by the bed. The wind maker dodged the first attack then parried the next. The third attack was his and it caught Thryn completely off guard and sent him head over heels onto the bed. Griz's clavus came to rest on Thryn's neck.

"Calwin, help," he said, desperate for assistance. "Cast a spell and we shall leave this place."

Calwin stood without moving.

"Calwin! They will kill me! Don't you love me? After all we have been through. Don't let our relationship conclude on such disaster."

She remained.

"It looks like your potion wasn't enough," Khan said. "It wasn't courage that you needed. Do you know what you needed?"

"Calwin, please. Throw a spell and we will live together. I will give you everything that you want. Whatever you want tell me and I shall find it and offer it to you. I live for you. Don't let my life slip away so easily."

She ignored him.

"First, do you know what I needed?" asked Khan, eager to speak.

"No."

"I'll tell you. I needed a potion – if there is one and I don't think there is – to remove my beliefs. That's right. Remove my beliefs that a thief could be trusted; that one who only cares about himself and zorn can be trusted with anything as valuable as a friendship. Do you know what friendship means? Do you? Because I don't, but I'm learning."

"And what is it that I needed, Khan. Humor me whilst a clavus rests upon my brow."

"You needed love." Thryn scoffed at the sound of it. "But there is no potion for love. Discovery is how you find love. You earn it, nurture it, and protect it with your own love. You have not known love. Without love, courage, strength, and all things under the sky are meaningless. They are, I tell you." He glanced at Calwin with a sad eye.

Calwin shook her head slowly from side to side but could not express with words her regret, red tears spoke instead.

"Not even zorn can buy love or loyalty," Khan said. "Not everything is bought by zorn. But you did manage to buy a very special gift that I now share with you."

Khan eyed Griz who took his cue and hacked down into the thief's torso. Griz raised the clavus again and chopped off Thryn's head. He would have struck a third time if the clavus head hadn't buried itself into the flooring and prevented him.

"That's enough! He's dead."

Calwin embraced Khan and kissed him passionately.

"I wanted to go back," she said to him. "I tried to but he wouldn't let me. We were running for our lives. I missed you so. I thought you were dead..." She kissed him repeatedly. "I thought you were dead..."

"Forget it. You are like the rest—an expensive prostitute."

"Hey!"

"I'm not finished! If there was a choice between a batier at my chest or you, I would choose the batier. At least the damage from a strike can heal," Khan said.

"I didn't love him," she said trying to explain.

"Too bad. It might have served you better."

"Where's the wealth?" asked Griz.

"It's gone."

"Gone where. Did it disappear?" asked Khan.

"It's gone."

"Where?" asked Griz.

"I don't know where. Probably in primo and prostitutes. I never saw much of it."

"No, of course, not. You were too busy having sex with the other officials," said Khan.

"Morb!" She slapped his face. "I love you."

"Don't worry, I won't kill you."

"Does this mean it's over?"

"Yes, Calwin. Finally, just when you're beginning to understand me our time is up. Relationships always end up like this. There is one more thing that you will do for us first. You will clear our names with the guard. I don't know who put it up but you will use your political friends to clear this up. If not, you will die, I will see to it and you know that I can do it." She looked at Thryn's corpse and got the point. "If you don't want to end up like that then I suggest you talk to your friends today."

"Okay, but that's it."

"Once that is done, you can go back to your own life as long as you stay out of mine."

Khan grabbed her bracelet and Thryn's ring, and him and Griz walked out.

AS PROMISED, Calwin removed their names among criminals and by the second day Khan and Griz could walk the streets again as if nothing happened. She convinced herself that it was in the protection of her life that she did him that service but really she knew that wasn't the truth. It was for the love they once shared. A scent that never fully went away.

Thryn's death was marked down as an accident and it was also found that he owed a lot of others zorn with which he had been living off of, quite extravagantly in comparison to the average wealthy entan.

Khan returned on the third night after following her back to the inn. He had persuaded himself to come though was not sure why he wanted to in the first place. So much time together with Calwin and so much time lost, he thought. I love her but I cannot love her. She and I cannot be together and it is funny because if all things were perfect, and they aren't, we could be together but we are on different paths and have only met it seems at the crossroads of our lives, and while I move to the east she will go west or south or maybe north I do not know. I do not care to know. She is aware of where she must go.

There arose another pain in his body and this time he could not trace its origin. He questioned his visit again and then decided that it would be better to go through with it rather than fail at this point. All he needed to do was to maintain his composure as he saw her one last time.

She was packing.

"Are you leaving?" he asked.

"I'm moving to the twin towers," she said, unhappy at the thought.

"Ralwindale's towers."

"Yes. Tomorrow, he will leave this urba and will take me to Ravada."

"Your life improves."

"Please don't leave me, Khan," she said. "I am so sorry. I made a mistake. Many mistakes. I want to stay with you."

"We are not meant to be together," he said.

She stopped packing and threw the case off of the bed.

"But I love you," she said while sobbing.

"I should go." He could not bare the repressed emotions any longer. Lutas have always been better with emotions than lutos.

"Don't. Please."

"Griz waits for me."

"Why did you come? I don't want it to be over."

"I just wanted to say good-bye. I should say at least that much."

He headed for the stairs. She ran out haphazardly and grabbed him with both arms.

"It cannot be over," she begged. "It cannot."

"It is," he said and looked into her sad eyes with his own one last time.

"Khan! Don't leave me like this!"

"We could have had it all, but we didn't, did we? Look at you, Cal. You are smart and beautiful and all the things that could make any luto happy. I hope that you find that settled comfort you seek. I could not provide such tangibility. But you know that now. You never understood me, Cal. You never tried. I think if we failed in something then it was in understanding each other."

"I understood you."

"You think that you did, but you were too busy trying to satisfy your own wants."

"But it doesn't matter—I love you."

"It does matter. Without understanding, what do we have? How do we please each other if we don't even know what it takes to do so?"

"We had love, Khan. We still do."

"And now you have found another to love."

"No, I do not love Ralwindale. But I cannot be alone. Take me back and I will try to understand you. I can learn."

"I am pulled once more into the future, Cal. And where I go will be to a place of wonders unlike any wonders that I have already seen. There I will find my life and my death. I feel that."

"Take me to that place," she pleaded.

"It is too late for that," he said.

"No, it's never too late," she said with words he had used before.

"It's late...and...we must part..." He pulled himself away.

"Khan!"

He showed no more sign of love or affection and shielded himself to their invasion.

She pulled at his clothes ripping them in several places as he continued.

"Shev'la Khan, I hate you! Do you hear me? I hate you!"

Khan reached the bottom of the staircase, leaving Calwin midway in screaming tears. She remained there holding tightly to the railing as if the railing was the only thing keeping her alive. Only then did Calwin face her own seedishness and how her own actions had led her to this point and that only forced her grip to tighten.

Shev'la Khan stopped at the bottom of the stairs, the sobs from Calwin echoed in his ears and discomforted him. He adjusted his clothes and his smile as he walked towards the front portal to where his friend awaited him.

Griz asked: "Are you fine?"

"Fine. Let's move."

"Are we clear?"

"We're free," Khan said. "Born again."

"Then it's time for a couple of fresh primos."

"I'm glad you said that."

Calwin's sobbing continued to echo in his head until the noise of the crowded and snowy street overcame it and the two adventurers immersed themselves into the body of entans roaming the urba. Action among interaction.

Minutes later, only the little purple sack could be seen and then even that blended in with all the other colors of Seranor. Casus, the urba of adventure and mystery, was on the economic rise.

Chapter 3

ALEXANDRUS, KOZOTIAN seed of Remlan and Zaran
Scaeval of House Scaeval in Reinor, did not enjoy his
luxurious, well-brimmed life; tio after tio turned
time, wasted in a body with a bulging waist.

The advent of a developed financial and monetary
system in Seranor left his own family fat with more
wealth than they could spend. He accustomed
himself to lounging around the castella, constructed
of hand-carved lutium plates and designed by his
father's cousin, Yest, an absolutely lazy Kozoty if
there ever could be such a thing but a brilliant
creator nonetheless. The castella was larger than
most of the other Houses and usually empty inside

save for the evening parties where those of the new wealth would come and exaggerate their spoils; only to fatten their extended bellies and bottoms under the grand image of Duality: two intertwined snakes playing with a white sphere nearly the length of forty entans, if put head to foot together in an arched line; the largest painted ceiling from Anjapo, the artist.

Alexandrus, or Alexan to most, was calm and highly intelligent though relished dressing in expensive and tailored clothes so much that it became a necessity. Alexan spoke with precision and all his opinions contained strategies of efficiency and economization. His decisions, since his youth, had an exactness to them, but family matters proved to be his creative challenge.

At the time of his last argument he could not contain his disgust for his father and could not understand the reasons why his only remaining parent enforced his will rather than reduced it.

It was not uncommon for his protective and militaristic father, Remlan, to demand certain requirements such as training with the military spear, mastering the long batier, and wielding arvicity. He took to the lutium batier early; first developed by House Levin whose entire family innovated military equipment. The batier had evolved since its birth as a strictly bludgeoning weapon made of cross-hatched, twisted cora fibers and later contained rings of lutium that cracked surfaces, and porcelan for that matter, very efficiently.

Alexan tinkered with his, improving both design and mastery of the flexible Seronian weapon, even experimented with pliable lutium compounds. His current batier was 3 centimeters in diameter, 70 in length, and had one centimeter rings laced through to the core every 10 centimeters of equal spacing except for the end where two rings were separated by a distance of only 3 centimeters to increase damage as the head whipped to strike an opponent. Alexan often carried his batier with him and it was sheathed behind his right hip. On the long hilt was a small engraving, hand-carved by Anjapo himself.

Arvicity to him was uncomfortable as it used the planet's energy rather than restored it. There was no choice in the matter of learning arvic manipulation. It was the skill of House Scaeval and his father was reputed to be a great arvician on Seranor, one who had paid more attention to zorn than of arvicity in recent tios. Still, Alexan practiced the steering of the planet's primal breath without the dedication his father demanded. Remlan blamed his seedling's laziness on the home comforts and only further insisted that Alexan focus a meter more than he did. Alexan complained of the life he preferred while his father reminded him that he was still a naïve seedling born of position and not of will.

These military things he did to keep his father pleased and satisfied, in turn, his father allowed him some indulgence in time spent outside of family interests. So he ventured into the forests outside of Reinor to study with his friend, Pala-del, an Aktavion, mortal kol and protector of the land and of cora. She was once part of House Kel-Abda, but managed at an early age with lenient parents to satisfy her interests. Aktavions were found all over the planet, hidden sometimes in regions yet untouched by entans, places so remote that even the dark-shelled morb didn't willingly cross.

But life had taken a strong twist, as of late. Recent days were more deplorable than previous and yearning for the chance to demonstrate his own ability to himself, he had lashed out at his father and made his demands. He wanted to study to be an Aktavion, environmental protector like Pala-del, his friend. Interest had blossomed into occupation.

What he expected and what he received were the same – his father wouldn't allow it under his dual-colored eyes, key Kozotian traits. He decided, hastily as possible, to leave the House of which he could never return.

He lay on the soft cora grass in the furthest yard of the castella, now plump and scared with displeasure, when he remembered what he had said to his father just that morning and tried to sleep it off without effect. His mother recently died of a strange illness and was what triggered his own desire before he too succumbed to an eventual and unpredictable death without the satisfaction he so desired.

While outstretched on the soft lawn on a hill overlooking the mountains and beauty of the land, a young acolyte named Burrard came by, curious at why Alexan was there. Burrard was still at the age to be curious about things and to see the simple joys of life. He had always lived in a nearby forest only choosing to come to the urba when he needed supplies. There was an innocence about him that reminded older Kozoty of what life should be like and many of them did not want Burrard to change for that reason. So he remained.

"Alexan, why are you like this?" asked Burrard.

"I am listening. Listening to the land. Listening to her song," said Alexan, picking at the tender cora grass chutes. "Listening to my life…watching its moments…"

"But I have never heard her speak, the land, I mean to say."

"She always speaks. Sit. Listen."

The young Kozoty sat down.

"Listen carefully. Close your eyes. What do you hear?" asked Alexan.

"The beasts." Burrard paused, closed his eyes and took in a breath. "The trees," he said, finally.

"Now, what is behind the beasts and trees?"

"The wind, I hear the wind blowing between us." A hollow wind had come by between the two of them thrusting the ends of their clothes about in a soft whistle, slightly pulling at them and drawing them to wherever it was traveling.

Alexan defocused his eyes for a moment, carried by the fresh current of air. "Yes, better. Now, see through the wind's disguise. What do you hear?" he asked.

Burrard listened intently. "Still the wind," he replied.

"You must listen more often. Next time, try to have two open palms on the cora—Have you seen Pala-del?"

"She is readying to leave—"

"For where?" Alexan asked, raising his voice in excitement.

"Casus."

"Why does she go there?"

"How would I know such things?"

"You and Pala-del have been friends for many tios. Do not hold back such information that I wish to know."

"I don't—"

"Burrard?" said Alexan, rising his head with intonation.

"There is a meeting there," said Burrard, quickly and abruptly. Alexan raised his hand and extended his finger and waved it side-to-side signaling his dissatisfaction for the exclusion of details. Burrard rolled his shoulders this way and that and said: "That is all I know."

"I must find her. Where is she now?" Alexan wasn't satisfied. His life of luxury had ended from the moment he left and now he searched for the one thing that could soothe him.

"In the urba buying supplies..." Alexan had already gotten up, running for the urba a couple of kilometers away. About 100 meters on he stopped, thinking that this was incredulously futile, recalled a long distance flash spell and bopped off. When he reappeared the second time, he had already reached the main road. Arvicity had its benefits.

The shopping in the square took Pala-del extra time. The packs were all full on her brownish talin along with rope, aqua flasks, and a large flat piece of luggage strapped on at the front. Alexan came scrambling down the road she was on though she did not see him in the busyness of the crowd as she called out her talin and mounted it.

"Pala-del!" Alexan called for her attention, waving his arms more frantic than he'd done for a long time. A hand of acknowledgement waved him to come over.

Still breathing heavily: "Where are you going?" he asked.

"To Casus," Pala-del replied, more out of habit than anything else. She was older and more experienced that Alexan and had felt somewhat responsible after influencing him to become interested in her profession. At the time, Alexan was burdened with his father's demands and sick mother. Had she been thinking responsibly, which she mostly did, she would have let the young Kozoty wrestle through his own misery certain that he would survive but there was the glint of desire in Alexan's eyes that reminded her so much of her younger self that she succumbed to his pitiful disposition.

"Why?" he inquired, eager to know more.

"Why do you ask, Alexan? If you must have the specifics then it is about a meeting that awaits my participation."

"What meeting?"

"An important meeting," she said and stopped with a direct look in his eyes. Alexan didn't want to listen.

"I want to go with you. Take me along. I can help out and do whatever is needed. I must leave this place. Can you understand? My father and I have recognized our differences and now there is nothing for me here so you must let me join you or my life will be over and all our time together will go to waste. I will be ready in two minutes, as soon as I get a talin. Agreed?" He spoke firmly like his father, but with an exaggerated confidence to make up for his seedhood, then ran again to a young Kozoty mother who had just dismounted her talin. A verbal exchange took place. Alexan handed the female Kozoty a shiny object as she handed him the reins. It was tall-shouldered and black-hued. He pulled it back to his friend who was left waiting without a chance to reply.

"Next time, don't do that. I hate it when you push others around, Alexan. I hate it even more when you push me around," she let out in a rush.

"I apologize this time but I must leave. Father will not accept me and I can no longer show my face around here any longer. I want to leave. I want to reach Casus. I am ready to go. Can we ride together?" he said with that pitiful and swaying look upon his brow.

Pala-del stared at him briefly, closed her eyes in an effort to blind herself to what she was about to say and then said it. "Let's ride."

The ride out was peaceful. Two talins, one brown and one black, carried two figures blackened by the brightness of the land. She never spoke of her meeting and Alexan, feeling fortunate at his situation didn't ask.

Travel over Seranor especially from the protected area of Reinor was more vacation than venture. Alexan didn't so much like it as he had seen the area before and felt no threat from the land or its inhabitants. He did look forward to Casus, not so much for the urba itself, but more so for the distance it would put between him and his father.

The second and third day it rained ice balls double the size of a Kozoty's crystal-shaped eyes and they lost some time waiting under the shelter of trees.

"You have left your family, Alexan. A family is all that we can keep in this life," said Pala-del.

"Family."

"What is it that you have against them?"

"They prevent rather than support. They force rather than attract. They earn rather than express. If this is family then I have no need for one," replied young Alexan.

"I know that you have had your differences with your father, but your father is such only because of love and of knowing things you don't."

"All he knows is his own method that he wants me to happily digest. A seed is not a piece of clay that is meant to be shaped by fathers. It shapes itself, does it not? If he loved me, he would know that more clearly."

"Love blurs more than it binds."

"I am full with his demands."

"And what will you do now? What will you do in Casus?"

"Be free to choose what I choose, to think my own thoughts, to carve my own life. As you have done, Pala-del. I want to be an Aktavion and to protect the land."

"Being an Aktavion is for all but not all are for it. There is much to sacrifice."

"I am willing. You were fortunate that your parents were far more lenient than my father. My mother was understanding before she left."

"I was sorry to hear about her passing."

"She was most important in my family."

"There is something that you should know, Alexan. Something that I should have told you before."

"What is it?"

"I don't know if I should tell you…"

"We have been good friends for so long…"

"Yes, but you may not like to hear this."

"What is it about?"

"It's about my parents."

"They also didn't want you to go?" he inquired.

"Yes and no. You see, my parents…my parents died some time ago, seven tios before, in fact. Those two parents, lenient as can be, you have seen were bought by my family's wealth to fill as figure heads to their fortune and estate. I have no mother or father any longer. Seranor and Seragorn, if anyone,

are now my parents. They are my real family just as
Seranor is the mother to us all."

"You did not reveal it to me before."

"Some pasts are best left quiet. I only tell you
now so that you don't make the mistake of losing
your family under the wrong assumptions.
Everyday I miss my mother and father. Everyday.
At least your father remains."

"To think of him burns a hole in my cerbind. He
forces me to do things I care not to do. I want to be
an Aktavion like you. Is that so much to ask? He
wants me to study arvicity and to become an
arvician like him. A great arvician, I am not. It
takes much more than I have to be such a thing.
And to what end? Arvicians only consume the
planet's limited resources. What is the purpose in
that?"

"You are free to choose. Not everyone is so
fortunate. To be good at any endeavor you must
believe it. You must digest it with all your love.
Sorry to use the digestion analogy that you so hate.
Are you willing to do this to be an Aktavion? Before
you answer, consider it.

"I once wanted to be an artist to add beauty and
expression to the land. My mentor and inspiration
was Anjapo. I lived and breathed all that he did and
when he stopped and moved into the trees to live as
a pilgrim, I was so discouraged that I too stopped.
My life changed in those moments of rest. Before
that I was so preoccupied with Anjapo's work that I
only had time to eat and sleep. I was so far behind
him you see. Instead, I became what I am now not

because of my choosing but because of life's choosing. It chose me far in advance of me choosing it. In a way, I am still expressing this artistic value to the land. Now my paintings are of a different nature altogether."

"You wanted to be an artist?" asked Alexan.

"I was a good artist. Some said that I was a great artist."

"Then why become an Aktavion?"

"Because that is what I should be. And if you want to find true fulfillment in your life, find out what life wants rather than what you want. Take out the thought and decision is made easy."

"How will I be able to do that?"

"Seranor will guide you with her subtle hand."

"And if I make a mistake?"

"Then she will knock you hard so that you stop to analyze where you are and what you are doing. There is no wrong choice really."

"And if I don't hear her?"

"Alexan, you have learned to listen to the land, have you not?"

"Yes, you taught me—"

"And how did you accomplish that?"

"It took some time to retune my hearing from air to land. Vibrations were so—"

"But once you adjusted everything, every sound became clearer, crisper, right?"

"Yeah, after I understood what you said then I could...hear her...just like I will know what is...chosen for me...my path..."

"You are still a long away from that."

"I know," said Alexan.

"Keep to your senses and you'll do fine."

Pala-del's skills as an Aktavion proved essential to the hasty travel the two undertook. She understood the forests well and found a safer route, slightly longer in distance, under the protection of trees. There were several close encounters with wandering morb that were avoided in the camouflage of cora. Alexan had only heard of these shelled monsters from stories and persuaded Pala-del to watch them from a distance before moving on. Dark clay shells protected their backs and joints. Thick hides, of petrified clay it seemed, filled in the rest. What Alexan despised the most, and what almost made him cast a spell at one of those morb, was their squat heads and black eyes that looked about in disgust and hatred.

The only real fear came from sighting a large troop of soldiers bearing the signs of the Ice Timor. Pala-del had been informed about their movements over the land. A larger formation split into three groups and one marched toward Casus. No matter. Two on trained talins moved swiftly and much faster than fifty armed soldiers. From that point on, the trip went by uneventfully. Alexan used his travel time to occasionally chat with his friend who grew worrisome as they approached the urba.

In Alexan's cerbind lingered the exposition she had released near the start and throughout their journey; he was certain that this decision, that to leave, was not made by his hyperactive cerbind, rather it was the default when his cerbind was overcome with desperation.

Chapter 4

THE ICE Scabbard was full again on this dark and rainy evening. The rain, half ice and half aqua, beat down on the streets like an attack of ice shards on the flesh. Storms had become more common around the planet. Rain, a normal phenomenon, and other weird occurrences such as land shakes and drastic drops in temperatures with a moment's notice came unexpectedly and more frequently. None knew with certainty why the weather, always consistent and predictable, had turned against Seronians.

Some of the pessimists and the doomsayers, Aktavions would agree, said that Seranor herself had her hand in this for she was in pain and was crying out. These notions were laughed at by the majority who held the belief that everything changed and sometimes weather went astray. Ice and cold indeed had increased its influence from the center of the planet. The realm of ice had widened and those who went to explore its reasons didn't return. Soon it became dreaded by the common entans and the place marked with adventure for the others. The more danger, adventurers believed, the more wealth that waited for them.

By now the Sints, crusaders of Zorath, had marked their territories clearly; that struck fear in entans and gave confidence to the morb and the cerbors who found their way into urbas without the resistance from the Seronian Guards as once before. The Guards, in fact, welcomed the inclusion of others, probably on their side.

Entans of position and influence were often found dead in the mornings as they read the palpazine, the daily elos. Granida Kespoar, a rich entan investor known to have poured zorn into obscure technological inventions and the founder of the palpazine as a form of mass communications was found with a severed torso in his residence. Granida was a thick luto but the killer blow was estimated to have been done in one quick motion. Some were even found dead reading an article about their own death like Mala Opp, a speaker in the town square who spoke of nilospace and celestial negation. Questions and concerns were never answered properly and inquirers disappeared quicker than they could ask for some answers. The Seronian Guard became suspect with Sint influence within its ranks. Trust, as it was once before, was dwindling fast among ceramin. Eventually, questions about the dead, dying and the damned were no longer asked.

The daily palpazine used the elos, elliptical language of Seranor – drawn characters that were arranged in a spiral formation read inside out – and delivered in *nods*, small whitish spheres of palp. Palpazines became widespread and contained all the essential of information Seronians required on a daily basis.

Data embedding devices were developed to mass produce the palpazines, printed on flat translucent cora sheets that were rolled into hand-sized nods for mobility. A command softly spoken in gud released the nod into a larger sphere of information which would then open sections, much like the lifting of leaves on a branch, whereby the reader saw the elos projected in the air in front of them, and still able to see through it by focusing and defocusing. Articles were all viewed this way and Seronians enjoyed their mornings with the only planet-wide palpazine, QUERIST.

Between deaths, weather changes, Sint crusaders and morb, the rest of society was occupied with the making of zorn. Numular councils were standardized in every urba and, business after business, Seronians became wealthy. Those of older age and eccentric personas took little interest in mercanomics. They became comparatively poor in a short amount of time. Some adapted, some didn't. It was a shakeout as clay dust falls through a sift and the meatier chunks of clay remain from where they came.

IT HAD been several weeks in fact since Khan last attempted to break the seal on Pyxa; his pride and possession still kept out of stranger's eyes in the purple sack found in the gray mist of the tomb that he and his new brother had emerged from, emotionally pummeled, but intellectually unscathed; lonelier nonetheless.

He called Pyxa a she mainly because of her radiant white beauty and the warmth it brought to his emptiness. He always carried the sack with him even when he slept. Griz harassed him about it at the beginning, but with an attention span of a rain drop, the friendly lug gained more interest in anaprimo and scoring his lucky number, 51, of course.

The edges to the cylindrical Pyxa were smoother than the best porcelan skin, warm to the touch like his mother's hand when he was sick and dying as a seedling. Oh, how it reminded him of those he had lost, and how he tried to cleanse the milk of his past.

When placed on one flat end, Pyxa stood exactly 18 centimeters tall and 13 centimeters at her diameter. A long, intertwined serpent with multi-colored scales was engraved in the middle portion not taking more than the widths of two fingers pressed together. A song played as he brushed his fingertips along the snake's coiled body. Above the

serpent was a carved drawing, etched into the
material itself, on a red background. The vivid
colors depicted a summarized episode of an unknown
past. How vivid they were those colors. What of
color? thought Khan.

Khan recognized the central Kozotalian figure
wielding phosphorescent multi-colored rays with its
very eyes, arms outstretched with open palms each
containing an object. The objects, a mountain and
river, were much more miniscule in comparison to
the real size or perhaps the Kozotalian was
supremely large. Too subjective, he thought.

A gigantic serpent glistening with eternal
charisma brightened the background like the love
that pours from a mother's corius. To the backside
of the figure was a colossal avian creature, black as
the abyss with eyes of red and a open beak emitting
beams of absolution. To the bottom of the engraved
snake was a white background with two serpents,
one red and one white, stretched end to end and an
oversized bright white ball between them. Just
beneath this drawing were the four glyphs of the
elements, equally spaced out on a semi-translucent
bar circling the entire object. Her name,
Pyxacognitartis, was hidden in the engraved
serpent, between its scales in an ancient elos known
to a very few.

Khan found an art teacher, Jaspron, in Casus
who he felt provided the ideal opportunity to study.
At first, it was because he hoped that the teacher
might help him unlock the mysterious object.
Ralwindale, the one he had met, was a fake and the

authentic knew nothing of what Khan spoke of, and so, discouraged, he found friendship in the kind Jaspron.

The young teacher taught art in Ceramin's Square every second night shortly after the bright hues of Seranor calmed. It provided the right setting for his classes and many locals would come to sit, talk and listen to the theories of art. Even Khan started in such a way before befriending Jaspron and spending more personal time with him. Time was an excess commodity to the wind follower with zorn as a luxury.

Jaspron, full name Jaspron Valducian, was plain in the spirit of the Casus. While most lutos geared up and bought a cheap map to some unknown treasure site, Jaspron chose to inspire society, for better or worse, in his regular teachings. Art was fast becoming a lost set of knowledge with technology as its replacement. As one of the cornerstones of Seronian thought, art was an integral part of history that many, in their tios of peace and boredom, were learning to forget.

All art used color and color was math. It was the highest form of math seen by the cerbus as an impenetrable language of maximum construct. Subjectivity was at its core. The inventors of color – the Kozotalians – invented it for a reason not unlike the reasons that adventurers run after what they see in their dreams. Reasons provide base motivations for interaction which was the underlying purpose behind the construct of pigmentation and the animation of all life on planum Mettadi-di Flamma.

The Kozotal, through perfect bodily compositions that permitted all things to bloom without filtration, cast about the psychedelic hues of mass saturation and the illumination of the planet from which they themselves created. Vividness and vitality flowed brilliantly enabling the creation of all things meant to be without hindrance or disruption. And beneath such bliss was hidden, as an intertwined numerical song, the crux of the Versos.

Jaspron was tall as most with exceedingly long black hair that stretched down to the small of his back. He kept it twisted up and to the right in a finely carved cora stick making him look like a piece of art himself.

He almost always wore a bright smile as if his cerbus was permanently tapped into a vein of joy. This positive aura he shared with his students and it gave his classes meaning uncommon in other lectures. His Kozotian father, a drummer, and half-Kozotian mother, a dancer, brought him up in Svein, a port urba in the northwest region bordering on Mare D'Albatus.

Jaspron's parents forced him to indulge his creative spirit rather than subvert it, and this focus, especially in his early seedhood, enabled him to revel in the truths and tastes of art. While others were keen to make a living from trading artworks, Jaspron enjoyed sharing the knowledge he had, but he did try to become a numularian of sort at the onset and failed miserably.

From Svein, the Valducians traveled, as a benefit from working in the creative realm, and after spending time in Gaze and Zahara they eventually ended up in Casus where Mr. Valducian diverted his drum talents to the Sonian Healing Institute (SHI), the largest healing center in the urba. Jaspron married soon after but his wife, Pali, died from an extremely rare red milk disease that corroded her bone structure. Two tios later, Jaspron arranged his learning sessions in Ceramin's Square and the combination of his dedication and expert knowledge quickly earned him a reputation.

While Khan and Jaspron built a mild friendship between them, Griz absorbed himself in his own destructive habits. The multiplied strength of the armored warrior, fed by his chain girdle, coupled with his unpredictable rage, made him into a feared phenomenon in the urba. Every week, at least two bodies died by his hand and it was Ira, rather his secret operatives that remained faceless and nameless by his order, who bailed him out and prevented him from getting further in trouble.

One, two, or three murders could be solved but Griz was indefatigable and his rage only grew so Ira had no choice except to spread the word that the angry luto was best left alone and witnesses stopped speaking after the first two or three were assassinated for their dutiful contributions to the Seronian Guard.

Ira could not fathom the two of them, Khan and Griz, together as brothers, and thought it was some obscure and absurd joke played by the tail of Seranor herself for only she could be capable of this level of fascination. He strangely cherished Khan and had no choice but to involve himself with the uglier duties of watching the plated bruiser. And true to their relationship, Khan and Griz remained though in the urba spent their time largely apart. Khan researched in art and Griz diluted his milk to soften the raging noxy inside.

AS MUCH as Jaspron and he discussed things, Khan could not prevent the return to the understanding of art. The two of them talked, often after a lecture when everyone had returned to their residences. What remained in the atmosphere after an artful discussion was like a cloud with which they could drift up and above the norms of the day and the realities that so many depended upon.

"Art is mathematics," Jaspron blurted out after being unable to convince Khan that mathematics was intimately connected to art. Khan disliked math and what Jaspron said next stiffened his entire body up straight as if a long spike had been thrust into him from bottom to top. "It is the purest form of numerical theorems."

"No!" Khan yelled out, trying to break out of his immobility.

"Yes, my friend. Shapes, colors, angles, images, backgrounds, and scenes are all the pieces of math. They are the infinite numerical language form upon which the whole Versos speaks and breathes.

"Theorems of math are the reasons of interactivity. As you first told me when we first met that your father once told you that inventors, like himself, only manipulate numbers stretching them so that they may find the holes within which knowledge is hidden from the rest of us. This is much like drinking anascal if you are an arvician. Your father was a master mathematician who somehow managed to release the creative spirit. And the whole time he never realized it. That might be why he was so inventive. Lute like those are rare, Khan."

"They have become extinct." Khan breathed out in disappointment. "But Jaspron, what is art really about? You have defined it but I'm missing something and I cannot fathom what it is."

"According to Kozotalian legend," Jaspron started, "art was considered to embody the transformation of pure mathematical theorems into multi-colored art works. The works of art personify numerically-based theorems and all of their infinitesimal details. This is why we still – today – incorporate and follow art as one of our foundational thoughts."

"The Nivians never learned art and yet gained the ability to create. I have seen this—" Khan said.

"Not to create…well…perhaps from one perspective, but more specifically they learned to destroy. The very opposite of creation."

"This is the point I fail to understand."

"Nivians decided to keep and contain the purity of math. They did not realize, and still do not, that purity is in the expression. Pureness comes from the release of a contained idea. The ice realm did not believe so; therefore, they decided to purify in the reverse. Their planet and manipulations are based on this. It is why their power is greater than the Kozotal in control and destruction, in theory anyway. Creation, on the other hand, is only channeled through their theories, and though inventive, could never match that of the flamma world which conceals it in vividness."

"Conceals? What are you suggesting? That color is not really there because it really is just math personified in some calligraphic sense?"

"You do not see it yet, do you, Khan?"

"See what? The connection between art and objects?" Khan asked. Jaspron nods thrice in agreement. "Is there one?" Another nod, this time just one down motion and then Jaspron produced a small, many-colored box not much bigger than his hand, placing it on the ground they sat on. Khan had seen it before in his lectures so immediately brushed its top with his fingers and picked it up examining it closely. "What is there to see? I see an object in front of me."

"All these things I have previously said: image, scene, shape and so on. All of them are not there."

Khan laughed. "If they are not there then where are they?"

"Nowhere."

"Now you sound like my friend..." He was referring to the late Equist Nao. The last time he saw him was in the cellular acceleration device just moments before him and his friends all were slated to die. Momentarily puzzled, Khan asked himself, why is it that these teacher-types speak so simple as if they had been served a bowl of clay dust?

"True art, Khan, is an hallucination." Jaspron gently took the box away from his perplexed friend, rotated this way and that and as if an instantaneous spell had gone off – none indeed had – the many-colored box became a sphere with a uniform soft gray skin covering it. "Color is the mirage with which art paints. They exist only in our eyes." He handed Khan the now gray ball.

Khan grabbed it from him, slightly angered by his own blindness. Nao often said things like that to him and he had been slow to grasp those as well.

"We see them because we want to," Jaspron continued. "We also don't see them because we want to. Have you ever wondered why some colors are brighter on certain days while others are not? Well, I will tell you why. The color does not change. Our perception of it does. Our simple belief that one object is old makes the color fade a shade lighter than it appears to others. The same principle holds true for those brighter days. The cerbus, Khan, the cerbus is at the helm to keep things as we want to see them. To keep us believing that we are still in control when we are not. Control is not in our capacity though we sometimes wish it so."

"Then our society, our whole society is masked in color. There are colors in all places, products, and devices. Are they false then, too?"

"Yes. To some degree, they are."

"All of it?"

"Yes."

"Then what is real?"

"Much is real. All is real. Illusions are real. It is the color and the shapes of real art that fool us. They are the expressions of math. Of complex theorems that the entan cerbind could not understand. You understand? Adjust your vision and you will see through them. But first, you should focus on this small box before attempting to remove the curtain from the lives of Seronians. Keep it."

"Why?"

"Because the real image or shape, if you will, is not a sphere and though I see it, you still do not. That is why I am going to let you borrow this gray ball. It will clear up the haze you hold."

"Is there a cosmic purpose to this illusion? Why are all things masked?" Khan asked, bewildered and slightly agitated at his failing.

"Unlimited freedom," Jaspron started, "the intangible device we surround ourselves with, is only made unlimited in art because it is the illusion that allows us to dream, and in our dreaming all things can, and will, be. How can I explain what wasn't meant to be explained?

"We need art. Without art, without color, we are dead. And though this economic system stampedes into our lives, I fear that one day it may replace art and its wonders. What are we if not the realization of our dreams – of what could be and will be? Art, my friend, can open that channel."

The art teacher went on: "It is the cornerstone of Seranor because art cannot be defined and, in that lack of definition, art becomes all things to all beings. Unconstrained and uncontrollable. But after all has been said and done, color is an illusion, a phantasm, and to be able to see through its beauty you will see into its beauty until you yourself will become more beautiful, and only then have you truly appreciated what was meant to be felt instead of seen.

"Do not open your eyes to such things for doing so would not allow you to see it. Instead, open your corius and see with it, rather than your eyes. Use your eyes as the device of filtration and your corius as the one who gets the message."

Khan tossed up the gray ball with his right hand to catch it with his left. When his left hand touched it the ball felt somewhat different. He switched hands again and the feeling changed. And as what he sensed with his fingers changed so too did his perception of it. An illusion, he tossed the idea in his head.

Chapter 5

JASPRON WAS right, he found afterwards. Day after day Khan held that hand-sized ball in front of him trying to see through, in and around its illusion, and as each day passed so did another of the same. Nothing blatantly changed but he sensed marginal differences. Still no dramatic shift. The shape and color was the same as he had been given three days before.

On that third evening, a neighbor told him that Griz was facing another severe fight in a tavern on the corner. He had overdosed on primo. Khan immediately rushed over and found Griz surrounded by three morb. They were brown-black, armored in their natural shells, and they were ready to kill the piece of porcelan standing in the center.

Griz held his drunken clavus fast, ready for a fight to the death. Three or four other bodies lay sprawled in the tavern, busted limbs hung loosely and milk was sprayed on the walls. One of the bodies was definitely morb in nature and probably why Griz was about to get run down in his excess inebriation. Even Ira wasn't going to get involved with morb unless absolutely necessary.

What happened next was best remembered as a story that would be told to seedlings in the night when parental stories came to soothe the aches in their kols. The tables were the first to violently vibrate but the chairs and stools flew up into the air and swirled aimlessly crashing into other objects and splintering. It was an indoor ceramic snowing event that showered the morb who finally could not maintain a stable stance in the radical wind storm that had caught them. Griz too flew up and about, but he was pushed to the outskirts of the whirlwind whereas the morb were centered on it.

Ferocious winds, body parts and ceramic shards beat upon the protective shelled casings of the clay morb and when all was done no one could even remember that Khan had entered. It was his hand that raised Nata to save his friend.

Khan knew that Griz would not last the first melee round and the last time they had encountered morb they were more than a match. His wind skills had grown more succinct since then. This was special. In fact, he had gained the ability to control short gasps of wind to defeat an opponent by letting the opponent defeat himself. But this time

something different – wicked and uncontrollable –
came. From Nata's formless body, Khan twisted
himself drawing all her energy into him by reaction
rather then decision and in his own opaque desire to
save his friend, he released a wind fury that nearly
decimated the entire contents of the tavern.

The two of them had trouble walking the rest of
the way back to their residence from the spot where
Khan's wind gust had carried them. Khan knew
that something had happened. An ephemeral portal
had opened inside him and he had walked through.
All things seemed brighter, bigger, and better. The
air itself smelled sweet and not acrid like before. He
floated above the ground rather than touched it with
his feet and most things were oblivious to him such
as the ceramin who stared, the rain that fell, and
cold temperature that so concerned him a short time
ago.

In his high, he pulled out Pyxa, after rounding a
corner and not noticing anyone. The moment they
stopped, Griz's body collapsed in a pile of clashing
ceramic plates. The black girdle that Griz had worn
daily all of sudden shimmered green and if he didn't
have Pyxa to examine he would have certainly
pursued the girdle that provided Griz with
malkarian strength.

He pulled her forth from his purple sack and
looked at her. The images on the drawing began to
move and shift. After placing Pyxa on the ground,
she lit up. The topmost image danced and
characters acted out their parts. Rays and beams of
white and blue shot out between the Kozotal and

Nivian as the serpent and the avian beast battled. In the end, the avian beast was slain and the serpent embedded itself into the very ground. When all was done, and the serpent was gone, the Nivian and the Kozotalian faced each other and struck one another. Both disappeared. The once red background turned blue and the ground became white. Then after a period of nothing, a smaller-sized gray figure popped up and jumped out then over the engraved serpent at the center. When he landed, he joined the two serpents below who by now were still motionless.

The faceless and hazy gray being grabbed the white ball, held it fast and released a wave of colorful light spread out in a fan-like motion. Below this image, the four glyphs representing the elements glowed. The figure then looked at Khan and said, "When kol is weak, save mother. When mother is dead, release her." Then he too vanished and he left behind two vibrant and active serpents flowing side to side, playing with the glowing ball until finally one of them swallowed it. At that point, the elemental glyphs disappeared leaving behind a small riddle: ART SPEAKS BUT DOES NOT LISTEN.

THE PUZZLES of the planet. Puzzles were left to the creators to hide their craft and to demonstrate their wit even when managing such great forces in the world. Pyxa or rightly referred to as PYXACOGNITARTIS was actually composed of three main concepts.

Khan hadn't seen this before but now with his clarified vision he saw it: PYXA represented a box; COGNIT or cognition stood for learning or philosophy; and ARTIS was, of course, art or color. "The box of philosophy and art," Khan said to himself. Now, it looked much clearer than before. Only one problem: where was flamma?

If he was right to suggest that philosophy and art were the two then obviously one more was missing to finish the three cornerstones of Seronian thought brought down from the Kozotal. This was the box containing the essence of Seranor. What was that? Are the three cornerstones of knowledge that which makes the planet? And this riddle: ART SPEAKS BUT DOES NOT LISTEN. What does it mean?

Without further guesswork and after a quick glance at his snoozing brother, smirking at the full grown seedling, then Khan looked at Pyxa and drew a sigh. "I have lied to myself without knowing that I have lied," Khan said slowly as if speaking to Pyxa. She just sat and maintained a warm glow, an outpouring of emotion that made the windy wanderer cry. Even Griz smiled in his sleep. He continued. "To know that I feel you is to know that I was once empty and now I am filled." Khan stood there for several minutes more, not moving, not speaking, just soaking in the rawness of Pyxa before packing up and taking Griz back home.

In the morning, after the shock had subsided and his cerbus had settled, he awakened to a new day. He couldn't help but to churn the concept of art and color in his cerbus. Art had been present his entire life and only now did he notice that it closely represented Zorath. He could not have guessed that mathematics was hidden in the perplexities of art. He could never mention Pyxa to his art loving friend. He avoided it during their discussions but he suspected that Jaspron was not as young and naïve as many would take a teacher for. Teachers, after all, were the closest to mastering what they taught than those who practiced it. Nothing was fully learned until it was fully taught.

Why were shapes and colors numerical and not natural? It was logical to relinquish the esoteric value into naturalness. It was unacceptable for math to be part of any society. And it disturbed him that his inventive father did not make mention nor comment about such things except in brief. Had his father known more? Possible, he answered to himself.

Color was the first layer in the foundation of life. Living things all relished in the beauty of color. It was the inspirational natural art that motivated societal growth and development. The mirage that kept forward momentum forever moving forward.

Development, extension, adaptability, progression, and evolution were all terms used to describe the advent of entans and the proliferation of society since the birth of the porcelan being more than one thousand tios ago. All of these were precluded by the one basic precept and that was the brightness of color contained in the concept of art and concealed in the hand of mathematics.

Kozotalians knew of this also. They were the masters of art which later became one of the cornerstones of Seronian thought. But that is the cultural divide between Flamma and Ice. It is the difference that makes creation gifted with far greater potential than that of control.

Art is color expressed. Color is the raw material with which masters paint their worlds, and those that wield the brush, firm and gentle, as if aqua flows between their fingers onto the canvas, are the ones who can tap color's limitless containment.

Seronians had learned the basic craft of mixing colors and using it to enhance the beauty of the urbas and residences though only a handful could delve further into its well of mesmerizing captivity. The most famous artist was Ion Anjapo. He had long since retired from his craft but maintained a healthy appearance as that of a seedling, in fact, despite his more than 600 tios age.

Anjapo had settled himself into the tree land areas near Maffin and lived a quiet life, kept mostly to himself, and spent his days communicating with the elements whom he began to believe were the reason for his existence. His most celebrated works remained among the largest urbas and in the Houses of the north which included, among his many thousands, the Mogue, Serendipity in Seclusion, Seranor's Song, and his largest piece that was painted onto the ceiling of House Scaeval of two intertwined serpents playing with a phosphorescent sphere (Duality). Of course, Anjapo was also commissioned to perform custom pieces that were sold, changing hands as often as one moves from urba to urba.

The main rival to Anjapo's work was Beecon Looc, a ventan painter who painted everything in shades of black. Looc was believed by some to be greater to Anjapo since he was able to meld the varying degrees of black into beautiful art while Anjapo relied upon the spectrum of colors available. The two of them and their followers allowed art pieces to develop at a fast pace throughout the world.

Khan remained perplexed by the riddle of Pyxa. Of course, it made sense that art spoke since it represented mathematic formulas which told things what to do. It was a language of the most fascinating kind. Why did it not listen? Who would be speaking to it? Art was one of the cornerstones, the central beliefs of entans brought down from on high. How could it not listen to its ceramin? He asked himself and responded. It doesn't listen. It was never meant to listen because it is a tool with which to learn. The learning gives us the skill to create and to make and to visualize what can be and cannot be and this is why art cannot listen. No, no. It does not listen so it assumes that art does not want to listen as if it had a presence all of its own. It sounds like art is a being and not a piece of knowledge.

When things were created in artistic form – true artistic form – then the art piece took on a life of its own because in order to construct art the artist must invest a piece of them self. And so the best artworks actually contained an intangible portion of the artist, a shell that has been discarded, a shadow of its kol, an "it" yet to be defined. Something inside to give it life and yet it did not want to listen. It spoke because it was the imprint of an artist's desire which was, at the fundamental level, the act of communicating a variety of meanings to those who perceived it, and yet, beneath its layers of illusion lay the underlying principles soaked in the theories of mathematics.

So it speaks because it is living and it doesn't listen because it is an incomplete being incapable of learning; simply made to be a permanent reminder to those who view its message. "That is it!" Khan jumped up yelling. "Art is a permanently stored message to be communicated for as long as it is unbroken. Breaking it breaks the message.

"It is the painful reminder of what the artist, or that unidentifiable portion of the creative individual, was trying to say. The riddle must be trying to tell me that art is only a message; a complex, mathematical, subliminal and very personal statement, but a message nonetheless." His voice had trailed off into a murmur by the last line. No matter. No one was around to hear him. Not even Griz.

Khan took out Pyxa once more. He stared at her and the images came alive again until it ended with, "When kol is weak, save mother. When mother is dead, release her." Then the riddle appeared. Was it a riddle? Khan paused first then restarted. He touched Pyxa, her warmth penetrated his very milk and he felt as if his innards were instantaneously destroyed and re-created, and said: "Art is the message." He was pushed away ever so gently.

She cleared him so that he could see the reaction to his genius. An amazing effect occurred. The engraved serpent, encircled around the cylindrical object, unraveled itself and pulled its long, flexible body off of Pyxa's white flesh. Each centimeter it moved away, an equal length of its body disintegrated into the air. As each magnificent, colorized scale vanished, it left behind an empty blackened center, completely devoid of any markings.

Once the entire serpent seal was gone, Pyxa dropped onto its side and rolled away from Khan who now stood with the grin of satisfaction. A testament to his father's work. The top and bottom snapped apart, popping outward briefly before they were instantly pulverized.

A seed-shaped object, oval, in medium-gray, became visible after the dust had settled. It was evenly colored and had perfect dimensions: 15 centimeters tall by 12 centimeters wide at its thickest point in the center, slightly smaller than the first. The top and bottom ends tapered off by 3 centimeters and held another set of ancient elos at their respective ends. One of the elos characters read: Pyxacognit.

Chapter 6

KHAN PICKED up Pyxa's reincarnation, Pyxa II, and felt its flawlessly rounded shell. He was cool to the touch. The three corners of thought, Khan ran through his head. The first was Art and it was obvious to him now, by elimination, that Pyxa II was of Philosophy. It was the gray that suggested it. Philosophy existed in the neutral zone so that one may contemplate the ideas of the Versos without upsetting the balance in the world. The neutral was always represented by gray. A medium gray, not dull and not bright but always just right.

Why wait? Time was moving quickly. Ira wanted to meet very soon for another mission. The time was now to work on opening the next lock, if that is what it is, and to reveal what is hidden inside. Cryptographers, still in massively short supply, preferred the thrill of the chase, the need to cure curiosity as if it was a disease eating away at their cerbind; they existed for the chase and not for the resolution. Anxiety overtook him. He considered patience and after finding no relationship with which to keep it, he continued to resolve his need to know. Khan's luck lived in the space of another's pause.

Entan cognition was a palette of verse. Since the creation of entan beings on planum Aquanomicus, the Seronians have always watched and closely monitored their learning and development. The greatest pieces of knowledge were always held secret and maintainable. But many would consume anascal and make the ascension into their spirit world.

Seraniva secrets, as well as other forms of undisclosed knowledge, could never be learned directly or their learnings would not be held by the cerbus and; therefore, vanish into an afterthought. No, reserved information was only retained by the one method of communication known as elliptical transference. The influence of media materials such as the palpazine were evident but in its original state this was used in transferring potent knowledge amongst ceramin. It was a dance of verse that the Seranivas and others could not understand and did not care to. They guarded the gate of great knowledge.

On Seranor, it was the way of philosophy, true philosophy, as true art, rather than expert knowledge. Hidden in the depths of the dance were the immortalized steps that took one closer to perfection and higher in power.

Philosophy, the cornerstone thought of Seranor, was the channel of learning while art was that of beauty. Philosophy, in fact, stemmed from language and language from the mysterious, or at least up until this point in the historical stick of time. Like knowledge, philosophy contained great amounts of information and cerbal stimulation that when tasted fully across one's cerbind, that very knowledge, concealed, brought out the hidden depths of talent that lay dormant. You see, the greatest ideas ever created by any being on any of the three planets was not the obvious but the obscure. The obvious was an opiate.

The ideas that changed society, improved the lives in uncountable ways, those ideas did not originate in thought; instead, those ideas were drawn out of the crevices of the cerbind by subjecting the recipient to philosophy.

There are some things that cannot be said as if to say them would undo the benefits they would bring therefore ruining the purpose of saying it in the first instance, and philosophy was the tool with which to say such things. It was unfortunate, especially when viewed by the stronger philosophers, that philosophy and life was limited by the constraints of language.

The last of the cornerstones, flamma, still eluded the wind follower. Now, he knew that Pyxa II was of philosophy and of secret information hidden in the elliptical flow of philosophical conversation. Only he hadn't found its relation or relevance to Him.

The cryptic elos, engraved at the top and bottom of Pyxa II, revealed a short verse. At the top: I AM. At the bottom: INDISTINGUISHABLE.

Khan replaced Him in his sack. Patience was a better choice. He needed to further understand the philosophical world, to brew it in his cerbind until the dark clay was burned away and a clear broth could be found.

THE LIT chamber was painted in a deep red on all four walls, ceiling and flooring. In the middle of the room stood several figures with one of them slumped on a ceramic bench fixed to the floor. Around the base of the curvy red bench was a pool of white liquid with small objects inside, and more of this gooey stuff was dripping down from the bench obviously from the open wound the half-conscious figure had received. The luto, Wallian Von-zree, was plain-faced and average in all respects, nothing remarkable about him at all except for etching on his porcelan skin at the inner left of both biceps. On the left arm was a beautiful serpent wearing scales of various colors that glistened in the flamma lighting. A long and black horizontal batier was etched on the right bicep. Both hidden from view and now exposed by an armored luto, Oh, who held up the luto's arm so that another luto, much more grotesque, could see.

The ugly entan was deformed and even Wallian, a traveler and warrior in his own right, had never seen such disfigurement. The luto's feet were no longer feet but two clumps of ceramic meat like the base of a cora tree without the roots. His right arm ended at the elbow in another rounded-off piece, and none of these peculiarities seemed to bother him or hinder any of his movements. The deformed entan's face, an odd bluish translucence, had sharpened features and he was completely bald. Half of the left ear was missing as if torn away by force, and whenever his mood changed he massaged his ear.

Every time he moved his trunks stomped on the ground as a drum would before battle. The more excited he became the closer to death Wallian felt. Behind him were three cloaked figures that stood motionless and speechless. They were so still that there were no signs that they were actually living and breathing, but they were certainly imbibed with life.

The look in Wallian's eyes were fixed and unswerving. The grotesque luto, calling himself Denar'ka, had spent the initial several minutes asking Wallian some questions that Wallian failed to answer correctly and had left him in a state of near death after repeated beatings from the armored Oh who used a custom made batier with sharpened edges rather than the standard rounded ones. Each time Oh struck, the sharp batier gouged another piece of his handsome porcelan flesh. Tiny porcelan shards were mixed in with the milk. The questions were not difficult to answer. No, no they were easy but they violated Wallian's code of honor. It was evident to Denar'ka that the growing presence of these radicals would sooner or later cause more problems than he, and his superior, was willing to accept.

For now, there were more important things to do and was what brought him to Casus in the first place. Denar'ka ran the company Narcophalin. It was based in the urba and processed a strange perforated crystal ore, derived from deep icy sea beds, into crystalloids, a source of energy.

Wallian was caught when he used his modified tard device to infiltrate Narcophalin's communications firewall and was tapping into private information. Denar'ka knew the etchings to be of the TOS, Terium of Seranor, a growing group of anti-government and anti-establishment radicals led by the untouchable Ira Levin.

"The questions have been asked, Von-zree," said Denar'ka, calmly and quietly all the meanwhile slowly thumping forward and back. "What are the answers?"

Wallian's main focus was on breathing. His nose cavity had been caved in and the now the air pressed through with great difficulty and left him with a strong sucking sound. It was obvious to him that he was dying and he didn't seem to mind which was what concerned Denar'ka. A dead captive was useless to him.

"Feed him a potion," said Denar'ka. His loyal guard, Oh, took out a hand-sized glass cylinder filled with a greenish liquid and fed it to Wallian who immediately refused it. Without much strength, Oh was able to easily force it down Wallian's throat. "Good. Now we will talk a different way, Von-zree."

As expected, the healing potion regenerated Wallian's wounds to a satisfactory level though far from completely healing him. At least Wallian was able to sit up straight but found himself still caught in a complicated set of limb shackles which kept him pinned down to a sitting position.

Denar'ka faced him, thrust both arms down in a jerking motion. Immediately after that his right arm turned blue in color and became flexible like a tree branch. Wallian could already feel the cold heat from where he sat. Denar'ka moved closer as Oh grabbed Wallian's left arm and held it out. "I could kill you but that would leave me without my answers. But now you will wish that you had spoken to me as I had asked. It would have been better with an arvicerer but we are here now," said Denar'ka just before his arm extended itself in a long blue reach and touched Wallian's exposed hand. The porcelan hand instantly froze and Denar'ka pulled back. Oh followed up by dropping his batier on it and smashing the frozen hand into a thousand pieces. Wallian was left speechless.

"What information were you trying to find?" asked Denar'ka. No response. "What information?!"

"About the processing," Wallian said, apparently still in shock at the absence of his hand. Denar'ka reached out again with an extended blue arm and struck Wallian on the shoulder holding it fast for several seconds before releasing it. The entire arm of the captive radical froze and, sure enough, Oh was there for the dramatic shattering effect. Tears swelled in Wallian's eyes but he did not cry.

"Why?" Denar'ka asked.

No response.

"Is all of the Terium so stupid?" Over the next ten minutes of a one-sided conversation, Wallian's body was broken down into an inconceivable size until finally he was left completely limbless, at which point his body went from minor fribulation into total arrest, and he died as an amputee.

PHILOSOPHY ON Seranor centered around the nature of all things real and unreal. Khan became worried about the future of the planet as technology proliferated replacing tradition and possessing entans with a gadgetry faith, a machine doctrine without substantiation or reverence. Technomicon, the largest numularian enterprise, along with its line of convenience devices, branded as *enicoys*, was growing and substituting standard goods with utility items. The latest enicoy on the market, *Intrator*, was introduced at Expo T, an international event that introduced new technological gadgetry and sponsored largely by Technomicon or its associated enterprises. Expo T was put on every 20 tios, usually under the banner of one urba, and it highlighted the latest technologies to come from the company's R&D labs including everything from flammic lighting systems, sensitive self-filtrating windows, photon translators (PTs), energy storage technologies and communications devices such as the tard. Last show in Ravada, a lively urba centered between the Canyon D'Altu and Aqua Nefast, it was rumored that a new device was in development to replace the hefty and inefficient tard.

Expo T also included items of luxury such as the new Intrator. This was an advanced model of the original flashpod device used to transport small and inorganic objects from one central location to an individual household. Tulai Khan, the uncredited inventor of the flashpod, had created a device based on a flat disc to which goods could be received. It was nothing more than a round disc embedded with the appropriate flash glyphs that replaced themselves over a few hours so that one could get several uses out of the device everyday without problem.

The Intrator was made up of a large ceramic bowl 40 centimeters in diameter and 20 centimeters high. Deeply etched along the top rim was a line of glyphs that activated a number of functions on the device. At the bottom, fitted inside the ceramic shell itself was a flat plate of ganium, the arvic storage medium used in all devices. This gave the Intrator a decent and balanced weight to keep it firmly in one place. The extra weight from ganium was not so welcome with mobile devices but a company called Storanium under the leadership of Jawania Belldoz was working on a solution to increase energy storage and to reduce weight using the umber colored ceramic material.

The Intrator worked by speaking a command which activated a glyph. One of them released a flamma screen that enabled the user to see the actual object they wanted to flash over. Objects were still limited to a size not greater than the Intrator itself and had to be of a non-living nature. The enicoy was sold through every conceivable location and Seronians snapped it up like a fresh clay steak ready for eating. Technomicon promised the availability of other sizes in the near future.

On one uneventful afternoon, Khan had found spare time in his currently meaningless life and decided to take a break from trying to open his precious little Pyxa II. He sometimes fought with himself on whether to open the box or not. Maybe it shouldn't be open by him, he thought. Or maybe, he dreaded, by opening it he assumes responsibility for what was inside, if indeed there was anything or perhaps it was some cruel joke. But putting a locked box in front of a cryptographer was like putting clay in front of an entan starved ten days in a row. There would be little you could do to stop either of them and Khan became more and more obsessed with Pyxa II as solutions churned in his head.

He now picked up the Intrator and smirked a fast smirk as he recalled the inventions his father made and how little they had progressed forward. His father had invented the very device itself from nothing. That was always the challenge. Creating something from nothing even though nothing was a loose term that had several definitions based upon the amount of belief in reality. Could there actually be nothing? According to legends, yes. Beyond Nivata was the realm of nothingness where nothing could or would exist. And something? The something came from above Flamma.

Chapter 7

AS HE rolled these unanswerable questions in his thoughts, a young, shapely luta walked by with a unique scent that entered his nose and slowed the spinning inside of his ceramic skull. She stopped at a point just behind Khan's right shoulder and then, without warning, burst out into a wild laugh as if she had seen something of great hilarity. And her untamed laugh resembled that of a seedling's rather than that of an adult. It was that seedlike quality that attracted Khan; that and the fact that Unita stared far longer than usual at the little purple sack that hung loosely underneath his left shoulder. Khan's batier was always kept on the right rear hip, at an angle to the ground.

It was at the point of contact when she stopped laughing, as if she was trying to understand it. Trying to read it. Khan couldn't resist to inquire and that started a bizarre conversation between the two of them.

"What is it?" asked Khan, curious to know the reason for the sudden change in spirit.

"You," she said.

"Me, what?"

"You keep an oddity on you."

"What are you talking about?"

"Your little purple pouch," she said gently lifting her head in the general direction and smiling all the while.

"My—"

"You don't know how to open it, do you?"

Her name was Unita, nothing more, and she was a perfect white without mark or indentation and with breasts of supple size and voice to soothe the skin of a luto as a silky cora cloth covers a naked seedling in the night.

"What do you mean that I—"

"I shall tell you if you like."

He blinked slowly to see if the image would go away but hoping that it wouldn't.

"You should be told or you may never open it."

"…yes…but not here," said Khan, furtively. This was too peculiar to let up. "Let's go over there." He pointed with his hand. She just smiled and walked over with him.

"You know how to open it?" asked Khan.

"Yes and no," replied Unita, "but I don't want to talk now. I want to play. Will you play with me?"

"And the pouch?"

"I want to play now!" she wailed.

"Okay, let's play," said Khan, reassuring her. She instantly calmed down and led him around to taverns and stores and squares, and they indulged in primo, dancing, trying, listening, speaking, and all other things that could be done in the urba within a day's time. None of it was serious and all of it was jovial. Her enthusiasm for basic things initiated a deep-rooted response in Khan that brought forth that seedling he had left in Ulaq, left in the middle of that ice lake. He absorbed her playfulness and they played together. He even forgot to meet with Ira in the afternoon, something which he had never done. Ira would probably forgive him. The more time they spent together the more interesting Unita became and soon he found himself desiring her sexually. Not the prostitute sexuality that comes and goes quickly, but of that innocent first-time romance. Not since Calwin, some time ago, had he any inkling to mate with a luta.

This luta was special.

Everyone liked her.

Everyone.

Amidst all of the play, and as the darkness came, he was reminded of the pouch close to his chest and the mystery it kept. Unita promised to tell him more and so he took her to his residence for a more personal and intimate setting. Griz would still be out for three or four hours, maybe more if he'd already knocked himself unconscious from over-drinking in one of the local taverns but considering his reputation and his capacity for anaprimo, he was certainly still up and running.

"It's more about math and science than of philosophy, you know," Unita said, without Khan first having spoken a word.

"No, I didn't," said Khan, enraptured by her beauty and her laugh and her bosom.

"Philosophy is a science, a different kind of science, Khan," she said and held a prolonged giggle. "Philosophy is steeped in the content and methods of mathematical logic. Logic, logic, logic. It is unique because it can be quite general and quite abstract also. General and abstract. You see?"

"No."

She giggled again. "Remember this. Keep it in here." She pointed to her eye. "It might be what you are needing." Giggle, giggle. "Substance of data and substance of a message...are...the...same. They only differ in magnitude."

"How?"

She put on a serious expression and said, "I'll example. If I said 'all arvicians use arvicity' it is the substance of data. Now if I said 'Zorath is an arvician' then it is the substance of a message. They are made up of the same substance and altered only by the magnitude of their reality." Giggle, giggle.

"Okay..."

"Keep that in here," she said, pointing once again to her eye.

"In here," Khan repeated and also pointed, trying to understand her point. A small burst of giggles erupted and faded just as quickly.

He grabbed her index finger, mesmerized by her continuous charm, and had moved in close to smell her soft skin. Pyxa II fell from his cerbind. Unita squirmed this way and that just enough to make him chase her scent and not enough to discourage him from chasing. This game went on for several minutes and kept Khan in a blissful state and just as he was about to move in further she pushed him away and ran out the door laughing vibrantly as she had done before. When Khan reached the door the only image he found was that of a shapeless rainbow that carried her laugh for another minute more before all of it disappeared in front of him. He even tried calling out her name to no avail. Unita was gone and he wondered if she was ever really here at all.

He returned to his room sexually angered. The juices in his body had raged inside like a storm and now had nowhere to express themselves. A turbulent storm circled internally.

In a bout of haste, he pulled out Pyxa II and diverted his frustration onto it after he could no longer bear such distraction. "I am indistinguishable," he muttered, looking at the beautiful seed-shaped gray shell. This time he was charged and his clarity was above par. "Now, I see who you are Pyxa II," he said to himself. He remembered what Jaspron had told him before about

art. The kol was the only thing in the Versos that
was the same amongst all the living.

So if I am indistinguishable, then I am a kol.

Pyxa II represents a kol.

Any kol since they are all composed of the same
material as my father has told me many times
before. But Pyxa II cannot be a kol…or maybe it is
the kol of the art object from Pyxa. He is the being,
the artist, that implanted a part of himself into her
and what remains here is the manifestation of his
kol solidified in a gray ceramic, cool to the touch.
Cool because he has died or been frozen in form and
cannot be reborn or recycled unless I can set him
free and to do so I must break him free from his
binding for the message has been received and the
art destroyed to serve its real purpose: to get inside.
"Forgive me if I am wrong," Khan said to Pyxa II and
picked him up, still agitated from his failure with
the young luta, in both hands. "I will free you from
your self-sacrifice and you will once more warm the
nilospace with your creative gifts. I will reanimate
you! I am indistinguishable!"

Khan reached high up above his head with both
hands and cast down Pyxa II hard onto the ground.
The object spun around and horizontally hit the
floor. Pyxa II hit only once and stopped. Just as he
had predicted, the gray shell cracked and hot white
pressurized mist jettisoned out of the cracks. As the
shell cracked so too did the tension that had been
built up inside of him and he calmed down. As the
mist came out, the shell melted and evaporated until
all that remained was a hot and wet mist with a

glowing object sitting at its core. It was made fuzzy by the mist. Khan didn't wait. He reached in to grab it. The object was warm to the touch and much smaller than the first two shells he had cracked. The object of flamma had been found. Not a mark, nor a scratch was on this smaller object. It was a flawless white of a material not seen before. It was neither ceramic nor metallic but more dense than the two. It was small: 9 centimeters long by 8 centimeters wide and 8 centimeters high. At the top was a serpentine figure made of up a mixed entan and Kozotal. "Seranor's Box," he muttered. "The one thing my father...said..."

Running along all sides was an elos, ultra ancient, spaced evenly with one elos to one centimeter. Khan counted 34 characters in all. Studying several of them, Khan understood it to tell a tale of Seranor and Seragorn. Nothing else identifiable to the now weary wind maker. "Could it really be...Seranor's Box? What have I done?"

Khan glanced outside and noticed the quietness in the dark, and when he listened further through the open curtain he heard a familiar giggle like it was whispered across the mountain tops. Griz's heavy footsteps stumbled up the stairway. He tucked Pyxa III away safely and then decided to do the same with himself.

KHAN AND Griz were of the poor. Their limited wealth from their adventures ran dry and they walked around with nearly empty tards as the months dragged on. Griz had used most of his on number 51, his prostitute of choice, while Khan had to repurchase all the equipment that had broken over the last trip on top of living expenses. Casus grew more expensive by the week as the market developed and wealth increased.

Ira Levin, Khan's good friend and employer, now wore a blackish-blue suit of immaculately designed plate armor on which he still had the black batier. A few pieces of jewelry had found their way on his body also. And he was healthier than ever.

Khan, looking for something to do, traveled around searching with little luck. So he and Griz started hanging out at the Ice Scabbard for several days a week and it was on the third week that Ira and another heavily armored Kozoty entered. The second Kozoty wore a bristly white plate suit with a hand-and-a-half batier high on his hip. A mark, similar in attention to detail as Ira's, was proudly worn on the left of his breastplate. Ira spotted Khan immediately and called him over. Actually, he knew that Khan was there but wouldn't say. Griz, disinterested and dazed, joined the three of them.

"You are back, I see. Better than before," said Khan, obviously happy to see Ira again.

"Yes, I have been busy," Ira said. "And I didn't forget that you missed our meeting."

"I have missed you and your intelligence," said Khan trying to avoid the issue.

"Let's keep that between us. This is my friend Issachar Draconus of House Draconus."

"Happy to meet you."

"It is a pleasure to finally meet the cryptic luto," Issachar said, speaking in a more formal tone than Khan had grown accustomed to. His voice was deep and proud with a slice of arrogance that cut pessimism like a slab of soft clay. "You have assisted our campaigns in the past. We may need your dedication again."

"That was tios ago," said Khan.

"Yes, but your crypto-knowledge has only now been copied by those who oppose us."

"Thank my father for that," replied Khan, he tried to hold a smile for something his father had done but it slipped away lifelessly.

"I was sorry to hear of his death," said Issachar.

"Khan, I too am sorry that I was not there," said Ira. "They were dangerous days."

"Let me introduce, Griz," said Khan, trying to change the topic and at the same time including his most trusted partner. "We are a party of two looking for things to do."

"I have some things for you, Khan," said Ira.

"Something that suits you," said Issachar.

"Khan, we don't want another morb-shat adventure," said Griz.

"Who is asking you anything?" said Issachar.

"You want to make something of it, pretty one?"

"You would be a waste of my energy."

Griz stood up knocking his chair back. A gauntleted hand cracked open a fist-sized hole in the table. Issachar gripped the hilt of his batier. "Griz, Griz, it's okay, he didn't mean anything," said Khan, trying to rescue the situation before emotions billowed out uncontrollably.

"That royal cerbor insulted me!" Griz yelled.

"It's all right, there is no reason for milkshed," Khan said, looking at his friend, telling him with the slow movement of his eyes and the soft touch of his hand that it would not be a good idea to make these people angry. Griz knew that they needed zorn. He only cared about two things: anaprimo and No. 51. Both of which came with a bill and with his nearly empty tard he wouldn't be able to get either. It was Khan who reminded him of that. If not for his windy friend there would be a dead body, maybe two or three, on the floor now. "We're among friends," Khan said, reassuring him.

"I will go," said Griz. Khan pulled him to the side. "Tell that unmannered piece of white mud what I think of him later." Griz stormed out.

"Emotional, your friend is," commented Issachar, unexcited by the challenge.

"Only when words without care are spoken. He's had a difficult time," said Khan. Even he was beginning to dislike the thickness of this Kozoty's ego.

"Many entans have had a difficult time. The intensity will only increase."

"Enough instigations. Khan, there is something that needs doing, but time is short and two party members are insufficient – especially an emotional one," said Ira.

"Griz stays, he is my most trusted friend."

"He is full of noxy."

"I can handle him. His strengths far outweigh his weaknesses. And we all have weaknesses, do we not?"

"Fine," Ira conceded "but you will need two more for this next mission. Do not worry about the third as I have just the luto you need. This mission requires a thief of sorts."

"Listen, Ira, thieves and me just can't work together anymore. I'm sure that I can do most of what is necessary, the rest we can improvise."

"This time will be different than before. Technological devices have evolved and are increasing the demands on us. You will need one and you must accept the one I provide. It will only require your cooperation for a couple of weeks at most."

"We can't cooperate. We coagulate."

"There's much more zorn in this one than any previous tasks you have taken."

"How much?"

"Plenty, I'll tell you later when your team is together and operating."

"Fine, the thief just better be reasonable and keep to himself or it will get ugly."

"But you still need a fourth, and it must be one who can use arvicity at least to some degree."

"That will take some time."

"You have until next week to find one. Meet me again in one week. I will introduce the third member and you will bring your fourth. Here is some zorn to start your preparation. Do not buy weapons or armor, only purchase the equipment you need." Ira handed him a bulk credit tard with extra zorn not attached to users and that could be downloaded into personalized tards.

"Thanks, I'll start right away. What are you here for, Issachar?"

"Just here for a friendly visit," he said, smiling.

"Right."

"What say we forget this talk and indulge in some fine drinks," Ira said.

At the tip of the morning, Khan returned home to find Griz sleeping on the floor. He was still armored and was holding a tall empty flask. It wreaked of anaprimo, the cheapest kind.

"Griz, what the farck are you doing?" No response and Khan was too tired to move him. He just dropped into his bed to sleep and threw a cora blanket over the armored hulk.

They rose at roughly the same time in the afternoon, twenty-past-two to be exact, he told Griz about what was happening and they decided to advertise for some positions. They posted a memo on the tavern walls and the occasional one in the street. It read, '*All those with arvic skills and an interest for adventure, bring your spirits and your selves to the large warehouse two blocks outside of the red district during the next three days*'. An address was attached at the bottom.

The two of them posted up nearly fifty posters all over the popular areas in Casus expecting enough applicants to find the right one.

"Well, it should be simple enough to find one arvatist," said Khan.

"There must be hundreds waiting for adventure," said Griz.

"Let's hope that luck finds us this week. In the meantime, we must start preparations. Ira has given me some maps to study but we need some equipment, I'll tell you the specifications then you can buy them with this tard."

"Back to adventure. I can taste it already." Griz took the tard handed to him and they parted ways. The ugly lug was reasonable without the liquid drugs.

Smiles ran across their faces as once again they were on the path of mystery and danger. Adventure, it was called, the ultimate Seronian drug that swapped risk for security, pain for protection, and the unknown for predictability. These were the true drugs on the planet and many were seduced by it. Many were exposed because of it.

Chapter 8

CASUS FINALLY appeared over the horizon and Alexan had woken with excitement. Pala-del rode for those eight days with a growing concern on her face but would not reveal anything to Alexan then nor now. He didn't care anymore for things related to his House or his family or anything for that matter, only relished in the fact that he had been released from his life of luxurious imprisonment. It was true, though he didn't readily show it, that he was scared of an uncertain tomorrow. What would he do? Where would he be? What would happen to him? No answers came to any of his questions and this struck a line of fear into him that he had never felt before. And the line began to lengthen.

By the time that Pala·del left him alone for good in the street, the line became a splinter running through him and he fell to the ground, dirtying his expensive clothes, crying uncontrollably. No passersby cared to soften his feelings; he remained in shock for several hours before gathering the courage to stand up again. The meeting time was approaching and Alexan had to find his good friend.

Alexan arrived at the agreed meeting grounds, Pala·del had not shown up. After waiting for more than one hour, he went in search of her to the location he suspected she was at. When he still couldn't find it, he pulled out a brush that she had given him and cast a simple spell to find her. As he was close enough he tracked her scent. When he rounded the corner after entering an old building his jaw dropped in horror. His friend and teacher, Pala·del, lay dead on the ground, naked as the day she had been born. Three openings, bored into vital areas, left very little milk on the floor. They were attacks of precision from one with detailed knowledge of the workings of the body.

He remained for some time crying over her. Besides his loss of control when they arrived, it had been many tios that he had cried but the sheer impact of loss had brought back old tears. By the time he left, carrying his friend's body, it was raining heavily outside. The drops of aqua were soft and warm and it soothed him. Washed his senses and his self.

Pala·del was buried in a field outside of Casus. The clay was soft at the top of a small hill and he

chose this spot to bury his Aktavion friend. Soon the
rain washed the existence of a grave and she
returned to the elements.

His clothes by now were soaking and dirty and so
on his way back into the urba Alexan entered a
nearby tavern to get a drink. It was fortunate that
he did not reach the Ice Scabbard then because when
he made his demands upon the bartender three
roughly hewn lutos led by a loud-mouthed cerbor
approached him and beat him senseless, taking all
that he had except his nice suit. They left him in the
street with nothing else save for dripping milk from
his damaged face. He ripped his own clothes to wipe
himself but was too weak to move for several days.

By then a stern look found its place on his face
and, though weaponless and poor, he summoned all
his skills and made a roughshod spear from a broken
down residence. Then he recalled his teachings in
arvic manipulation and practiced until some
proficiency was maintained. And then came the
promise to himself. He would not return unless he
succeeded on his own and would do what was
necessary to reach that. No one would strike him
again as long as he had his cerbind intact.

Brown clay marked his clothes and his face
matched his expression. He felt dirty so found the
public bath and washed his body clean, free of
charge. The clothes, torn up and stained, would not
come clean but he tried his best before putting them
on, dry, again. As he walked along the streets he
saw a poster on the wall asking for an arvicity user
who wanted an adventure. He laughed the first time

he saw it then he saw it again and took a closer look. A second laugh came but by the third he stopped and continued to read. It read, '*All those with arvic skills and an interest for adventure, bring your spirits and your selves to the large warehouse two blocks outside of the red district during the next three days'*.

Today, it said, was the last day for interviews. He decided to give it a try. Maybe fate was giving him a call and he needed to answer. Life was given a chance to take a new path.

THE FIRST and second days were no shows. No one came to audition so they rechecked the posters for errors and seeing no problem they reconsidered their strategy. First days were slow Khan and Griz decided, and it was best to wait until the end of three days. Someone was bound to show up.

The third morning, Yaryo came. Griz was throwing around his giant black clavus that he had purchased. One hand wielded it with a calm ease. The young luto walked with dark triangular glasses and Griz couldn't help but to laugh losing the clavus into the table where Khan waited. The table cracked in two catching even Khan by surprise.

"I am Yaryo. Arvatist and slayer of Malkar," said the young luto.

"Remove your glasses, Yaryo," Khan said.

As he removed them both Griz and Khan saw that he had no eyes and no sight. Khan's face cringed. Griz laughed harder.

"You handle it," he said to Khan quietly but his deep voice could not be quiet. Yaryo overheard.

"Handle what? My blindness, is that not so?"

"No, no, it's the table. He was referring to the table," said Khan obviously lying.

"Your poster did not say blind or not blind, smart or not smart, whole or not whole. I am equal to the rest if not better."

"I'm sure that you are, but we require one whose sight is clear."

"Fight me and I will show you my ability."

"This is an interview not a fight. Show us what you can do."

Yaryo put down his backpack, rolled up his sleeves and stretched himself out for a few minutes. By then, Khan was getting impatient but thought maybe, especially from the intensity in Yaryo's warm up that maybe this luto had something to offer. Griz even stopped to look seriously. Yaryo slowed his routine down, drops of fresh sweat slid down his face.

"I'm ready!" he said confidently.

"Continue."

The arms moved in arvic-like gestures, the body turned and moments of time became ultimate suspense until finally at some peak moment a spell was released and it came forth from both his hands a bright flamma burst. Khan shielded his eyes. It appeared instantaneously and disappeared instantaneously. Yaryo collapsed.

"Shat." Khan ran over to the unconscious luto. "Griz, he blew out an organ or something. Look at him."

Griz was already laughing.

"Good thing we didn't fight—Hey seedling, wake up." He slapped his wet face several times then when he saw a response he dropped him to the ground.

"Do I get the job?"

"Do us all a favor. Change your profession." That was enough to start Yaryo talking about his life and his hardships. It turned out that he was given away by his mother to live with her sister. She never paid much attention to him or his blindness and Yaryo took to listening to sounds. Over his youth he developed a knack for healing the injured by playing the drums of Sonians, sound healers and doctors. But he could not heal his sight for it had been too long. Too long unnoticed so he took pleasure in helping others before they became sick. It was when his aunt kicked him out saying that the planet did not need sonians, natural healers, it needed arvicians. And that was how he came to his new profession. Listening to all of this made Griz sick and he had left as Yaryo started but Khan was compassionate to those unrecognized.

"Yaryo, take some advice from me. Each of us has a gift to give to the land. Your gift is not to be an arvician. It is to heal the sick and dying. We may yet need more of you. Do not only look at the needs of today, look at your own needs," said Khan with a hand on his shoulder.

"My own needs?"

"Yes. Look within yourself and when you find it, hold on tight. Never let that something go. It is what separates us all and may one day keep us together."

"I guess I don't get the job."

"Another job awaits you. You're overqualified for this one. Get lost, will you."

He got up, picked up his glasses and held them in his hand briefly then threw them toward the wall and walked out.

Several more candidates had come by before Griz returned late in the afternoon to the warehouse. As he entered there was a burned taste in the air and large holes in the walls, as well as part of a collapsed ceiling on the floor. Khan had reattached the table and sat head first into folded arms on one end.

"You okay?"

"Huh?"

"Are you okay? What the farck happened here?"

"Don't you mean," Khan started laughing as he talked, "why are there so many holes in the warehouse or are you asking if I'm okay physically or...?"

"It's just a simple question."

"Do I look okay? We've got one farcking day left and after Yaryo, I had three of the wildest applicants I have ever seen. Two of them are over there." He pointed his hand to two dead bodies on the ground.

"There dead?"

"They're farcking dead."

"What the farck happened?"

"One came in – I think that one on the left but now I forget – anyway, he came to show his power and then the other came in. He seemed to recognize the first one, they argued over who should get the position – one threw a spell, the other defended and on it went until they were both where they are now."

"They also blew out the ceiling?"

"The ceiling—that was from the third lutoid who thought that he could manipulate a high level spell to impress me. I was impressed, impressed enough to kick his fat porcelan ass, and he was rather oversized, out onto the street."

"Interesting day."

"Tomorrow, you're going to stay around and watch." He placed his head back down on the table in frustration. Griz came over and leaned his clavus handle onto the table. Suddenly, the table crashed down with Khan falling into it.

"Farck!" he yelled then jumped up in anger. "It wasn't fixed. I just laid it together so that I could have what felt like a table but could not be used like a table…"

"You're not suitable for this job."

"I hate it! I hate it! Put me in a trap of death. Throw me to a Malkar. Give me a hundred morb and I will slay them all but take me out of this farcking place! If I see one more farcking arvatist or arvician or one more farcking idiot, I'm going to…"

A strange luto walked in unnoticed. "Is this the right place for an arvician to find a job?" His voice was higher pitched than normal and when Khan and Griz turned around they understood why. It was a luto no older than 15 tios.

"Yes, but you're too young!"

"But I can do all that you require."

"Sure seed." Khan looked at Griz. "Another lutoid. You handle him."

"Okay, what is your name?"

"Nibal Yek-key. Call me, Nibal."

"Nibal...what can you do? Show us something. Impress us."

The young luto had barely moved one of his fingers when an area in a two meter radius erupted in a spherical wall of blue flamma. "Throw something at me!" He spoke with uncommon confidence. Griz grabbed a small piece of the ceiling and threw at Nibal. It evaporated on the blue flamma. "Something bigger!" Griz looked behind him and found a large chunk of the table, nearly half of the lutium table that required four lutos to carry, and picked it up with one hand. He tossed it hard at the seed hoping to teach him a lesson. The chunk of table mostly disintegrated as it touched the flamma and several hand-held burnt pieces landed in front of Nibal. He relaxed and the spell vanished. It was after the first piece evaporated that Khan took notice and Nibal had definitely left an impression.

"Do you want to see more?"

"Yes—" said Griz.

"No!" interrupted Khan.

"No?" said Nibal.

"You are too young. The one we require must be older. It is this simple. Come back in five tios and if we are here we will consider you."

"But I can do what you require."

"Too young. You will have your chance later. The interview is over."

"But why?"

"I've explained it clear enough. The interview is over."

"But I don't under—"

"The interview is over!" Only from his wind reflexes did Khan save his life that day as Nibal cast a spell at him in frustration. It erupted at the other end of the warehouse destroying some old pieces of large furniture. Griz, slightly surprised, steadied his clavus for killing but Khan had already shifted to the young arvician and engulfed him in a windy haze long enough to make him sick with vomit. Griz came over with a big fist and crunched Nibal's body twice. Nothing broke inside. He held back. Then he picked him up, hauling him outside and threw him into the nearest prostitute house. He figured that a bunch of prostitutes would really send him home spinning.

"Good arvicians are hard to find," said Griz when he returned.

"It seems those that are good do not need a job and those that are not good cannot even pass the interview. And lutas are not interested in this sort of thing...We are in trouble. Where are we going to find a reasonable arvician? I'll take any arvatist at this stage. Give me someone reasonable. Someone with a little attitude but some class. Give me..."

"Hello?" asked a voice from the arched portal. "I'm here for a job."

"Will another applicant do?" said Griz to Khan.

Finding the two adventurers talking. "Timing is right. I saw your poster and am fit for the position." He was Kozoty. It was this fact that kept Khan's gaze more than anything else.

"And what is your name?" asked Khan.

"I am, Alexan."

"Just Alexan? No Alexan the Great or the Powerful?"

"There is no need to make laughter of my name. Just call me, Alexan. That is enough. What are your names?"

A bit surprised. "Khan, I am Khan and this is Griz."

"Not Khan the Merciless and Griz the—well, Griz the Grim..." Griz laughed and started all three of them laughing.

"Okay, Alexan, show us what you can do," Khan said, wiping the laugh from his lips.

"Over there by the half table, Khan?"

"Anywhere you like, Alexan"

"Have you been renovating?"

"Something like that," said Griz.

"The weather is not so good for it, you know."

A short laugh got out. "Thanks. I'll remember that next time," said Khan.

"Something funny?"

"No. Private joke," answered Griz.

Khan's head and shoulders vibrated. "Go ahead, start..."

"Oh, yes…"

Alexan moved arvicity competently enough without accident and after a few minutes of demonstration, Khan was satisfied and hired him. Griz felt neither here nor there with him. After a long day they all went to the Ice Scabbard for drinks. Alexan said nothing about his family; instead, he focused on his desire for travel and adventure. It reminded Khan of himself and the two started talking. Their conversation didn't really take off until they talked about things scientific. Khan was again impressed by Alexan's intellect and the two felt more like old friends. Griz was copacetic and didn't take much to the upper classed Kozoty: Ira was bearable since he footed the bills for their excursions. At the point of Khan's happy conversations, Griz just took to drinking more until he was well fried and lost his senses.

Three days' work done. Time for bigger things.

Chapter 9

SHOPPING FOR items had become interesting again. Zorn had that effect. Khan picked up an Intrator and used it extensively to coordinate the basic items they would need. Griz was left to run around and find the military pieces that he preferred. Ira was extremely generous, he expected no excuses to be put on the equipment, so Griz and Khan traveled to the shopping centers and bought from the best distributors. Many of their items were custom made and in limited supply.

It felt good once again to be needed. It mattered not where they would go or what they would do. That was the thrill of the surprise. The suspense that made all adventure euphoric. It wasn't for everyone.

Travel to strange places claimed many lives every tio. Where 100 fell there were 200 more to fill their places. Stories circulated about what was happening in the different urbas. Talk of Sint Crusaders spread like wild oxy and rather than putting fear into their lives, Seronians gained strength in the vitalization of society.

Laws, new laws previously unheard of, were being proposed in Casus. Rules to follow as suggested by newly elected leaders who felt it their responsibility to guide society in this economic and technological boom. As many locals were preoccupied with their new enicoys and flirting with the possibility of death on a new adventure, there were few to resist the governmental campaign. And, with passing thoughts, entans actually believed the leaders were protecting their rights which had become more complex in a developed society. Some of these leaders rose up from business and were successful numularians in their own right which somehow Seronians believed gave them a right to make larger decisions based on the fact that they could operate an enterprise successfully. Others found it strange that one who was familiar with production and distribution to be good at ceramin management. There were many obscure faces in the local government, some of them had never ever been seen, and still there were few who questioned the process. It was a combination of a lack of support, fear of assassination, inexperience with organized leadership and, probably more so the case, with general laziness from a slight dulling of their intellect as a result of societal gadgetization.

Prices for things, especially adventuring gear, had risen along with higher quality and better availability. It was on the second day of their shopping that Griz decided to release some tension with number 51 and Khan accepted his continued responsibility to finish the list. Alexan had promised to come out to help later on in the afternoon and would meet Khan at the Ice Scabbard.

Khan finished early, managing to store the equipment at the residence, and strode off toward the tavern by himself. The afternoon was slow and only a few bodies milled about. Khan sat by himself thinking about Mareenth and how she had left him. He still hadn't succeeded in his aims and was happy that she left for better things. His life, despite his optimism, moved forward slowly. He was getting excited, however, about the new adventure. Working with Ira proved to be interesting and dangerous at the same time. What ever happened to Nao? He wondered.

His wind training had reached a plateau and he worked harder to understand the storm that arose from within that time at the tavern with Griz. It was as if all that he needed or wanted or asked for came to his command without reaction or delay. It, everything, was there when it was required and as much of it that was needed. But how did it arrive? Did he just strike some lucky force with Nata's help or could, in truth, he regularly achieved this level of unlimited ability. Nao spoke of it before. To be hollow inside and to let things flow through. And that was why his skills had peaked. He felt like he had entered a new dimension in his training that moved from physical to the space between the kol and the real world. He wished that Nao was here to guide him. All of those he had so loved and cherished had left him though he did not push them away. Was that to be my fate? He wondered. So much to give and nowhere to put it. He wished there were baskets in the world that accepted pure gifts from those willing to give of themselves and each day the baskets would fill, and once filled could be poured back into society for those who required it. A dreamy idea it was.

KHAN DID not notice the small group of strangers that had entered the tavern. Three in total. The central figure was of the same height with a very handsome face. All entan. Alexan had yet to arrive. Khan thought it strange because the three of them approached him directly and he had never seen or met them before. The trio stopped abruptly in front of his table. The middle figure spoke first.

"I am V·Non, student to Denar'ka, of the IceFist. You are Shev'la Khan of Wind."

"Maybe."

"Yes. Me and my brothers – representing our master – have come to challenge you," said V·Non. All disciples of the ice used a name similar to V·Non to tell others that they were Nivatons, those who had achieved arkti state: body of naqui.

"Only the three of you," said Khan.

"I am aware of your talents, Khan. But the IceFist is stronger than the wind. We are superior."

"I have no need to prove myself to you. And I have no interest in it. So go bother someone else who will take the lot of you seriously."

"You insult all of us with your verse. Stand up and prove your worth in battle."

"Wind does not battle. We are the peaceful and the dedicated," said Khan, speaking to their faces and then to the walls. He had never liked this kind of competition, mainly because Seronians in general were not very competitive. The rising economy was changing all of that.

"You have had your warning," said the Nivaton.

"Thanks for the information," replied Khan.

V-Non and his two companions stood rigidly in front of Khan's table waiting for a physical act to transpire. Nothing. Khan drank his favorite drink and ignored them, but underneath the table his legs were ready to shift when and where as necessary. V-Non was not going to leave empty handed. Sure enough, the Nivaton struck at Khan who swiftly dodged the first three attacks from the enemy. The table splintered from impact with ice fists and the few eyes in the tavern adjusted their focus on the skirmish.

The three of them came fast and furious. Even Khan could not keep up the defense and was only able to make small offensives against them. They were far more resilient than he anticipated. The tables and chairs snapped and cracked like twigs under the power of the elemental foes. Three against one was not a duel but a death call, and Khan managed to stay relatively unscathed in the early rounds. His strength was waning and they were wearing him down which might have been their plan after all. Thrice the energy. He was destined to lose unless he could unleash that hidden force, that wind storm that now lay dormant. He called Nata. No response. His breath and his attacks were failing and he had received several damaging blows. Milk came from his face and arms. All of a sudden they stopped together and the two disciples, who had not spoken yet, stepped back six or seven paces while V-Non kept forward.

V-Non shifted his body and before Khan's eyes the Nivaton transformed to naqui. He forced the storm to arise, calling the unlimited power inside him and nothing came. The more he tried the further from success he went. V-Non stood in front of him and said, "Ice is stronger than wind!"

"Wind in your eye!" Khan yelled, attacking repeatedly with the last of his strength but in arkti state he had no chance to beat his opponent. V-Non lashed out and struck two blows, enough to throw Khan helplessly onto a table. As he tried to get up the table itself collapsed and further stunned him. V-Non leapt into the air for that final blow and as he came down a bolt of noxy seared his icy flesh and sent him flailing into the nearby pillar. Alexan had arrived. He followed his first spell with a more powerful ball of noxy that erupted on the two defenseless disciples and sent them running outside while afire. Khan hopped to his feat looking for a potion and remembered that everything was at the residence. By then, V-Non had recovered. He looked at Alexan, prepared to die in this fight, and Khan, near death before turning to the wall and crashing his entire body through it.

Only moments later, three cerbors wearing two red bracelets, one on each arm, entered the tavern catching Alexan off guard. A small battle ensued but Khan was too weak to fight and Alexan's arvic ability was no match for the cerbor's greater power especially since it was enhanced by his arvic bracelets. And while Khan was downed and beaten, and Alexan caught in a resilient hold spell that he could not dispel, the others picked one item from Khan's weakened and milky body, choosing not to kill him. They stole the bag that carried Pyx and ran off out the door.

Alexan recovered a minute later and went to help out his new friend who was washing his face with aqua, drowning his failure in battle. They were outmatched and out prepared.

"Does this happen often to you?" asked Alexan.

"You mean being attacked by complete strangers?" Khan said.

"Yes."

"No. There is usually a reason and at today's end I know."

"What is that?"

"My purple pouch."

"What is so special about it that they would choose to let you live?"

"It contains an item of importance. Of power, perhaps. I am not sure myself what it can do but do know that it has a part to play on this planet," Khan sighed. Another bad twist. "I must thank you. If not for you I would be dead for certain. Again I am happy to have you join us."

"I was merely looking after my job, Khan. Don't get sentimental just yet. With you dead I am out of a position. It is the position I need."

"True. Practical viewpoint, but true. I must learn this practicality. With you here now, I see we are adding some very different characters to our party. Later we will be joined by a thief. If that will do any good, I will be surprised. A thief. I just don't understand society. Would you hire a thief in your party?"

"Sure. They are quite useful. But I would not trust one to any extent. They are the selfish and the zorn-attentive. Their selfishness can be used to pry into places not possible by those like you and me. We all have our uses."

"I suppose."

The bartender came over to the two of them.

"Khan, that wall is going to be on your bill as is the rest of the damage. How are you going to pay—" asked the bartender.

"Take this," Khan said and handed him the tard filled with zorn. The bartender seemed satisfied with it. He had become accustomed to destructive occurrences. In fact, it was good for his business.

Rumor would quickly spread and other adventurers ready to get their heads smashed and their faces pummeled into the salty ground would come in hopes of meeting their dreams. He just didn't want to pay for it. By the time all of the damage was covered, all of the zorn was gone. There wasn't even enough left to pay for Khan's one drink, but the bartender let him off on that. He also said that he could come in for free drinks for the next week.

"I'm going out of town," replied Khan.

"Too bad," said the bartender from the back of the room.

Alexan and Khan, cleaned and presentable, walked home. Two blocks into their walk they encountered a large group of Seronians huddled together in the middle of the street. They casually investigated about the commotion. Khan was the first to see it. What he saw made him think much deeper than he had just. What he saw were the dead cerbors with the two red bracelets and beside him his two accomplices. All of them had two holes, one in their chest and one in their eye, that ran from front to back.

"Assassinated," Khan muttered to Alexan. "There is more at play here." The pouch was not visible. He could not be certain how it was taken or by whom but it was taken.

"What's in this pouch, again?"

"I don't really know. I don't really care anymore. Let them play with it. I don't want to be responsible for this farcking idiocy. We will soon have new items and treasures with which to indulge our lives. I don't need this. Farck!" He remembered all the time and effort he invested in opening the first two locks on Pyx. Taken from him. There must have been someone watching. He would have to be more careful in the future. Trust few, if any. Any of these locals here could be the assassin, he thought. He or she could be trying to set me up to kill me.

Khan was turning around, staring at entans randomly. Ready for attack that never came.

"What's wrong?"

"Nothing. Nothing," said Khan. He noticed the Seronian Guard coming. "Better not hang around here. I'm going to go. We will meet tomorrow at the arranged meeting place. Any problem, contact me on my tard."

Chapter 10

THE ICE creaked and moaned from within the walls and floors of the immense chamber in the ice station. Around the blued walls were eight well-placed and heavily armored synthetic guards. They were white skinned with traces of blue and translucent eyes.

In the center were six spherical areas of flamma all about the size of an entan's head but consisted more of a bright fog. Feisica-Sint, whose gift to outthink challenged even Nivians, monitored the influx of data from two of the spheres. The foggy spheres hovered two meters from the ground and a semi-transparent white figure, hazy at the edges walked around inspecting them as they provided him with deep sources of information that he worked to convert to useable data.

A large curved window made of clear ice was on the far wall. It looked over several mountains of white snow and cold ice. Zorath moved his left arm to touch an unseen panel on the window. His six-fingered left hand was black as was the arm that followed it, moving unnaturally to the demands of its owner. The black arm reached out to a point behind him that directly pointed towards the semi-transparent figure.

"Has the third phase been implemented?" Zorath said in a calm but low voice.

The figure, Kozo, flashed over. "Yes. As we speak, false leaders under your command gain the vote of the ceramin of the urbas."

"And the Arvinstrum?"

"Five have been uncovered, four of them we have. Another will return from Kolomir on the morrow. Only the last two remain."

"Obtain all the Arvinstrum, unlock Seragorn and we will have her."

"The entans, king Zorath."

"Entans are the smallest of my thoughts."

"I agree, my king. I agree. There are groups of them that elude our plans. They hide where we cannot find them and they strike against us. They are led by a Levin."

"The Levins—They are persistent to the end, these Levins."

"The underground organization – Terium of Seranor – spreads its web wider every day."

"No complication. A small infectious band cannot stop us when we have the pieces we need."

"Infections can grow or be overlooked, king Zorath."

"Unbiological," said Zorath and blinked a thousands ideas. When his eyes reopened a few had caught his attention. "We shall enact a new plan to control the masses. Control the disease that makes this planet." Zorath considered for a fleeting moment.

"What is to be administered?" asked Kozo, a Kozotal.

"Entans," he choked a laugh. "Their cerbinds are as malleable as cora and their intellect is controlled by their emotions. The pity of the Kozotal, they are. You know that, Kozo," Zorath said, looking at Kozo to hammer his position. "I will be the photon that will ignite the cerbinds of entans and their oxy will be their end. For it is in them to be supple to the power and knowledge and all things of greed. Greed. They have demonstrated such from our enterprising ambitions. The perfect race, hah! Technology warps their porcelan desires. Porcelan is the weakest element.

"I only produce what lute desire and lute desire all things that will be their end. And their end is nearing certainty," he raised his voice, clenching his black fist as if his worst enemy was caught in his hand. "Distraction is their weakness. Their cerbinds, flaccid as they are, will lose the desire for expansion and become completely satisfied."

"How is this to be done?" said the obedient servant.

"With Mediamenta," started Zorath. "Entertainment!—Tell our leaders to construct a lottery campaign. We shall call this campaign game Valuto, and will further drown society in their own rapaciousness. Allow entans to invest their zorn in adventurers and those of legends. Give them stocks of *oracles* – secrets to life – in each they invest and allow the stocks to rise for those that achieve success. Tell our assassins, thieves, and party underlings to keep Valuto interesting. Keep it volatile. Ensure me that Shev'la and whoever is with him directly is listed as one of the entan stock. This will keep the Levin exposed and vulnerable. Then we will see what rapacity buys. They will surrender themselves.

"And give them more to drink. Make anaprimo abundant. Weaken entans and the fight will be taken from them. Send our Sints to remove the small bands that surface, but do this after we have the Arvinstrum in full, lest we divert our intentions to quickly. For now, send the zoldiers into the urbas to create the seeds of terror.

"Prepare to begin the fourth phase. We shall not wait any longer. I have traced three of the points and you will find the remaining six. Soon we shall suck Seragorn from her mother's womb. Seragorn will soon rise, the planet will fall and I will have once again have what was taken from me."

"The zoldiers, my king."

"How are my creations?"

"Still in short supply. There have been delays from Vatu."

"Delays? Call Denar'ka to come here."

"He will be called."

"Tell him to bring me answers, not reasons."

"He shall be told."

"I will transform."

"I will inform you when he arrives."

Zorath strode out of the chamber, down a wide hallway and entered a dark cell. He stepped inside to lay down upon an ergonomic ice table. By the time his body was fully extended his kol had already left for its favorite destination, the nilospace. Zorath had maintained regular travel to the nilospace. In it he found comfort. He found home. A place he never had. He had met many of the existing kols in the nilospace and befriended them. It was they who first told him about the Arvinstrum and the artus locks. But it was Zorath who constructed the plan to usurp Seragorn's energy to weaken him for the final taking of the planet. In his love for his new home the Nivian had failed to notice something vital to his own essence as a being on Seranor. His body had become sick from his kol's extended leave and it was too late to stop the deterioration that had taken shape. The artificial kium arm caused him great pain to his dying Nivian flesh of ice, and he was already building a new body. A better vehicle to carry out his purpose.

THE HALLWAYS were three meters wide at the narrowest point, averaging a width of five meters, with circular open portals some four meters in height. All was made of ice crafted by the hands of master ice carpenters.

Transparent portals increased in opacity at a simple command until even the tiniest degree of difference was controlled depending on what was going on behind them. Smaller portals, round in shape and closed, were found anywhere from opaque to clear.

Sound did not bounce or travel at all despite the huge size of the complex. And it was always lit with a bluish tone from an inert lighting source.

A lone figure walked confidently down one of the long corridors. It was clear that his body was malformed as he lacked feet of the normal kind and in their place were shaped pieces of flesh like porcelan stumps. A rod of pointed ice, about the thickness of a forearm, made up his right arm. His face lacked the normal entan smoothness and instead of porcelan texture he had a rough translucence to his skin with a tinge of blue. A bald head matched the rest of his deformities, yet despite these malformations he walked straight and strong as any other with perfect balance and sense of direction as if these changes had improved his former self, rather than taken away from it.

Denar'ka's figure arrived at a large round opaque portal. Instantly, it turned completely transparent and, after a few seconds, the portal opened. He walked through, his stumps leaving a resounding thump on the floor as a deep coriatic beat in its final moments of life. The end of this shorter corridor resulted in an open chamber. Nothing was inside except two opposing couches made of softened ice. He sat, raised his hand and ordered a drink by simply calling what he desired.

Some twenty minutes passed when a hazy figure walked through the portal and as it walked it began to increase in form until a recognizable shape was assumed. Zorath had returned from his stay in the nilospace. His blue skin had turned gray in many places including his one good hand and much of his face. The left arm was now made of a supple black material, an advanced form of kium, and it moved with him just as all the other limbs. A look of distance masked his face. He took a few moments to gain his orientation and recognized the other presence in the room.

"This is the fourth time that you have come and the first that I call, Denar'ka. And it is the time I expect improvement," said Zorath, speaking slowly while sitting on an opposite couch.

"The factory is nearly at full capacity, my King. We are now producing 20,000 zoldiers a month and will triple production in three months. The third batch of soldiers were sent—"

"We received 90,000 zoldiers, but I want faster production, Denar'ka. I want an army in nine months capable of penetrating every urba and slaying the very army rising against us. Seranor's guardians grow in numbers and our numbers fall short from our main factory."

"We are at maximum production—"

"There is no maximum, Denar'ka—only invisible barriers. And you of all should know this! After all, it is you who has attained arkti state, is it not?" Zorath looked at the malformations.

"Thanks to you, my King."

"Send me more zoldiers instead of excuses."

"Our supply of crystalloids—"

"You will have what you need, but you must excel faster than your current pace or I will find another."

"Yes, my King," Denar'ka moved to get up.

"Stay. We have more to talk."

"Certainly."

"I have information on the location of the last two Arvinstrum pieces. They are not far from your ice keep. I will send two of my Sints to go with you to retrieve the pieces, Septana and Lavo, and you will keep them for a short time. As you will keep this box," Zorath handed him a small white box with an engraved serpent covering the topmost portion, the same that Khan once possessed. "Use your most talented to open it and reveal to me what is inside. Be careful not to damage the exterior and do not lose it or your life will go along with it."

"Yes, my King."

"A counter party is being readied to obtain the relics. They are no match for my Sints. They far underestimate my greatest creation as is the limit of their intelligence. You may find this of interest: A disciple of wind form will accompany them."

"An Equist, my Lord?"

"Not yet."

"Then he will be no match for me."

"Do not be so certain for he is gifted."

"Does he have a name?"

"Shev'la Khan."

Chapter 11

KHAN, GRIZ and Alexan met two days later near the
outskirts of Casus. Suspicion of political influence
on the ceramin was evident. Entans were afraid to
speak out as much as before. The center stages,
previously used to voice opinions and to discuss the
three cornerstones of Seronian thought, were often
found empty or filled with those who wanted to relax
and drink with others.

A new kind of ubiquitous drink, PRIMO NA, fit
nicely into the hands of the locals. It contained the
essences of anascal and anaprimo sweetened with
cora sugar and all mixed together with naqui·laced
aqua, just enough to keep it well chilled as it entered
the body. The drink was carried in a clear ice tube

15 centimeters long and 5 centimeters thick that
would melt over a period of half an hour. This kept
it always well-chilled with just enough soft ice
crystals inside so that it numbed the insides as it
slid down. Locals called it PRIME, as it both
energized a tired body and stimulated a working
cerbind for the next couple of hours. Soon every
shop, tavern and residence had stock on hand like a
new disease that spread into ceramin.

Strange cloaked figures were seen throughout
Casus and short but deadly battles were often fought
over the smallest things. Bodies fell and new work
was found as a Remover, one who removed bodies
from where they last lay. It was rumored by some
that two of the strangers were killed, stabbed
through the chest twice, but when their cloaks were
removed nothing remained but aqua. This struck
fear in the less adventurous who called the beings
Aquoids.

The biggest news was that there was an
announcement in the afternoon of today. A new zorn
making opportunity was being revealed by a popular
political leader, Oloomar Tyzan. He planned to tour
around so that all would have a chance to
participate. No more details were spoken about it
and this kept the anticipation high. Seronians
talked and waited anxiously on this new opportunity
to increase their wealth.

Khan was not so anxious about offerings from
Oloomar nor from any of the other leaders. Political
speakers had come seemingly from out of empty
space and helped urba dwellers so much that many

entans liked them and chose to support their future activities. It was a welcome exchange but Khan followed no one but himself, no matter what the benefit. He too lived by zorn, spurred by his wild youth, and felt it was the necessary thing to do.

The three of them met by an empty residence. Khan was late, as usual, but he noticed a blue-faced figure dressed in an overly long brown cora suit and while many would have brushed it off as normal he picked up something strange – he couldn't identify its gender. So he followed it. The brown-suited figure arrived at an older factory that had since been closed down and entered. Khan approached the nearest wall, scaled it to the top and positioned himself near a skylight.

Inside he traced the unused production devices covered in thick claydust, then saw some discarded clothing and repositioning himself he saw forty armored soldiers with bluish white skin and white eyes. He stared too long and one looked up to see him. He dashed to the edge, jumped off and ran towards his waiting friends. As he came running down the empty street his two friends waited at the end. He waved his hands up and down trying to alert them. Only sixty meters behind multiple footsteps stomped in his direction. Four soldiers chased after him.

"You're late!" said Griz, then he too saw what Khan was running from.

Khan stopped briefly. "Let's go." Then ran off again.

"Who are they?"

While running. "I didn't stop to ask."

They ran around two corners until finally reaching a dead end.

"Dead end," Griz said.

"I can see that," said Khan.

"Why don't we—" started Alexan.

"First you are late, then you bring trouble," Griz continued.

"Don't start blaming me, if it wasn't for me you wouldn't even be here. You'd probably be wearing those damn glasses…"

"So it is you I should thank?"

"Lutos! They're here," said Alexan as four of them came around the corner.

"Who should I thank now?" asked Griz as he readied his clavus and adjusted his helm.

"We don't want trouble," said Khan. "Who are you? What are you? Do you speak?"

In a flat and unemotional voice. "Underground rebels must die. All must die."

"That's my cue," said Griz as he lunged forward.

"Griz—"

It was too late to stop him. The clavus came down heavily, parried with a broad rader in the hand of the first warrior, but the clavus swung on its return and cut through its arm, severing it at just above the elbow. A bluish-white liquid burst out spraying Griz on his breastplate before he could move out of its way. Upon immediate contact the breastplate froze, cracked, and, as he moved, shattered completely leaving the hulk bare-chested.

The other bluish warriors moved in to fight and Khan and Alexan engaged them reluctantly. The skirmish went on for more than thirty minutes of parries, hits, and avoidance. Alexan's spells had only minor effects. They won only from the determination of their attacks. At the end all four of the warriors were dead and the three party members all sat down in exhaustion.

"What are these things? They are neither entan nor morb," said Alexan.

Khan touched one. "Cold, an ice cold with skin of synthetic touch. These are not natural."

"Artificial," confirmed Alexan as he touched one near him. "These are not from here. Their bodies soften as time passes."

"Ira might know more. Griz, help me to carry one."

Griz went to pick one up but as he grabbed an arm it came off and more of the liquid flowed out though without the effects of before. Then minute by minute the bodies all dissolved into aqua. And the three mercenaries were left stunned.

"Aquoids," said Griz. "Farcking Aquoids."

"We're late for our meeting with Ira," said Khan finally. "Move."

THE THREE mercenaries reached the location Ira and them were supposed to meet. It was under a gray overhang outside of a large round portal painted a dull orange with a handle at the bottom for rolling open. Ira was not there. They were ten minutes late.

"I told you, Khan, he's not going to wait," said Griz.

"Why don't you cool it, Griz," said Alexan. "We are here now and all we can do is either find him or wait and see if he returns to check."

"We should wait," said Khan.

"How long do you intend to wait?" asked Alexan.

"Why are you talking so much? You're lucky to have this job," said Griz.

"Lucky? Don't you mean that you are lucky to have me?"

"There are plenty of arvatists around."

"Really. And I suppose that's what you meant when you said that you were out of time and that you couldn't find any arvatists a few days ago."

"Your smarts will get you into trouble one day. Because if you always talk like this to me I'll crack your crown."

"Enough of this talk. Griz, we just hired him," said Khan.

"I don't think he's going to work out."

"Khan, I don't need this. I may not have a job but I have my dignity," said Alexan.

"What dignity?" said Griz.

"That's it. This overgrown tree trunk is just too deft for my acceptance. I would rather eat mud than travel with you," said Alexan as he walked off, certainly upset.

Khan ran after him trying to calm him down. Just then, Ira popped out of nowhere.

Griz jerked back slightly. "We're late."

"I can see that, Griz—where is Khan going?"

"He's trying to get back the new lutoid."

"The what?—why is he trying to get him back?"

"Because he got upset."

"From what?"

"The lutoid is sensitive."

"We don't have time for sensitivities."

"That's what I said."

"These are risky days. Call them back quickly." Ira pulled the handle on the circular portal and it rolled to the side opening into a well lit corridor. Khan and Alexan stopped when they heard the portal open.

"Get over here," said Griz. Alexan looked and Khan who looked at Griz who proceeded to go then Khan looked back at Alexan who loosened his tight-faced look and came along.

The four of them entered into a corridor. Griz shut the portal.

"Now, follow me," said Ira.

They followed him down two short flights of steps across an open chamber and down another hallway. Three portals were in front of them. Ira grabbed a seemingly random handle turning his head briefly. "Follow me. Twist left twice." Then he disappeared in a dim glow of light.

"Griz, go ahead," said Khan. He grabbed the handle but after several tries couldn't get the timing right. He tugged too hard and they heard a crack.

"Don't break it," Khan said.

"I didn't break it but farck this thing doesn't turn."

"Twist it twice—relax when you do it."

"Why don't you relax? Let's see Alexan do it."

"Happy to teach," Alexan said. He grabbed the handle. "It feels loose."

"It was like that," said Griz.

"Sure." He twisted and disappeared.

"Lutoid."

"Try again Griz. Ira is waiting."

Griz grabbed it again and after the second try disappeared and reappeared in small room. Ira and Alexan were waiting. The room was made of a dimly glowing material, probably a form of lutium, that provided adequate light without harming the eyes. Khan did not follow.

"Where is Khan?" Ira asked.

"He was just behind me."

"Wait here." Ira left the two. A minute later Khan came through holding a broken handle in his hand. The handle had snapped off, after already being broken by Griz's strong grip, and Khan couldn't get through. Ira led him to a secondary portal to get him down to where he was now.

"All you had to do was relax," said Griz with a smirk.

"Portal breath! You broke it when you went through," said Khan.

"It was like that. And don't call me that."

"Enough!" said Ira raising his voice. "We have more important things to do than to argue every five minutes. If you want to argue I suggest you leave now. Any of you who stay will shut the farck up and behave like rational entans. Is that clear! Now, come with me." Ira had never been heard to speak foul language and it was measure enough to listen.

They followed quietly into a larger chamber with similar walls passing many strange devices and lit areas. Alexan could feel that he was being scanned or probed but could not tell where it was from.

Sitting on a chair with his back to the group was another luto, as well as five lightly armed guards tending the exits. Large and small technological devices littered the sides of the room but in the center was a long shiny black rectangular table.

"Sit," said Ira. "Touch the table and it will serve you what you like. You just have to think of it."

Alexan sat first, touched the table and a glass goblet materialized. It contained a colored drink. "Haven't had one of these for a while."

"I'll take me a drink," said Griz sitting down.

Just before Khan sat down, Ira introduced the mystery luto. "Khan, this is Boon—"

Khan ground his mouth as he saw the familiar face when it turned around. "That farcking map seller!" It was the luto who stole his father's manuscripts and robbed him of his zorn. "There is no farcking way he is joining my party!"

"He's right for the job," said Ira.

"He's a thief, a scoundrel, the lowest form of mud on the planet. He will not travel with me."

"You promised to give him a try."

"Yes, but if you told me it was the same piece of clay that stole my father's last manuscripts and all

of my zorn then I would have said no. But you never
told me." Griz and Alexan ordered more drinks
while the others argued.

"I didn't know that you two had met."

"We met twice. There was some
misunderstanding—" said Boon.

"Misunderstanding? The only misunderstanding
was that I should have killed your dirty ass the first
time I saw you and I regret it now," retaliated Khan.

"Why don't you try to do it now?" challenged Boon.

"Keep talking, clay—"

"I'm ready anytime that you are…" Khan jumped
Boon in mid-sentence. Boon, with his expert agility
moved just in time to see Khan go face over with the
chair. He lunged again at the agile thief tricking
him with a double move and this time Boon went
flying off of the table accidentally knocking Griz's
drink over. Griz jumped up then when Ira extended
an arm he sat down and ordered another two drinks.
The two faced each other again on opposite sides of
the table.

"Let's just call it even and get on to this mission,"
said Boon.

"Not, until I have your hand," Khan replied then
drew his bastion.

Chapter 12

AT THE same instant that the bastion was fully drawn it disappeared and reappeared in Ira's hand. Khan widened his eyes in disbelief and it held his gaze for three seconds more than it would have under adventuring conditions where each second counted very lives.

"I have had enough of your shat today, Khan. You are going too far. What's done is done and your father is not here anymore so let's forget about what happened."

"Now there's a good idea," added Boon.

"And you, you kleptomaniac," started Ira, "if I so much as see you take a hair brush from him, I will personally find you and vaporize you. That's enough entertainment for today. Our time is already short, so let's not make it any shorter." Ira waved his hand for them to disperse appropriately into their seats as he strode over to the center of the large table. "Everyone sit!"

Boon sat a safe distance away from them all. "It was just getting interesting," said Griz with four empty glasses in front of him.

"I'll remember that," said Boon.

"As all of you know," started Ira. "The Nivian Zorath is extending his reach across Seranor and in so doing he is upsetting the balance of us all. His Sint Crusaders have struck fear in the ceramin. Morbs and cerbors inhabit many of our once free urbas. And leaders grow in the urbas gathering votes and supporters that some say are linked to Zorath but none have lived long enough to prove it.

"But the Nivian seeks something that he has almost completely acquired. He has scoured the land for the Arvinstrum."

"What is the Arvinstrum?" asked Alexan.

"The Arvinstrum is a set of devices last used to enslave Seragorn – one of the two cosmic Seragons – and to cast his energy into the planet. It is why the planet is here; Seragorn and his mother, Seranor – for which the planet is named – have kept the sphere whole and have allowed us to continue our battle to defend against worshippers of ora such as Zorath, but Zorath is no worshipper, Nivians are born of ora and know nothing else with which to judge life.

"He currently possesses five pieces, the first he already had and the second was found near the Inist island," he looked at Khan as if he knew all about it. Khan looked at Griz as if a secret had been broken. Griz returned a ceramic face. Clearly neither of them had squeaked a sound about it. "Anyway...the fifth piece was stolen just one week ago and it is why I have returned. Three days ago, we detected the last two pieces. It was easier because they were together and we implemented a significantly more potent spell to track them.

"Zorath knows of our discovery but we do not know how he gets all of his deeper intelligence. Know this, he will act with all his vigor to retrieve the last two pieces. We are already aware that he has dispatched two Sints from his ice hold in the mountains to retrieve them. What we need is a swift counter team to reach the devices first, get them and bring them back safely.

"Without all the pieces to the Arvinstrum he cannot succeed and as long as we have them, Seranor is safe. But you must bring them back. I cannot stress that fact. The Arvinstrum was our beginning and will be our end.

"The last Arvinstrum piece was retrieved in the urba Kolomir. A greedy numularian bought secret information containing the whereabouts of the piece. He then arranged for a stealthy mercenary group to take it and then had the skin to try to sell it to Zorath for one million zorn. Zorath sent two Sints with seven zoldiers and they decimated his resident mansion, his family and part of the urba."

Boon spoke: "And these two crusaders will be there?"

"Not if you arrive first, take the pieces and return," said Ira.

"Easy to say. What does this Arvinstrum do anyway? Can it hurt us, can we carry it, how big is each..."

"I expected as much from a thief." Ira continued. "Each piece has its own purpose. There are seven and they have names, of which I will not get into right now. They were created to rip the land apart to pull Seragorn out, to protect him, and to ensure that all went well in his binding."

"What do you mean pull Seragorn out? He's a cosmic seragon. A myth told to seeds to entertain them," said Boon.

"Seragorn is no myth. He is real. His serpentine body is intertwined throughout the planet and Zorath aims to pull out its head with the Arvinstrum—" replied Ira.

Boon: "Pull out?"

Ira: "Yes, pull out his entire head some kilometer or several kilometers long—"

Boon: "Several kilometers long—"

Ira: "Why is there always an echo in here?"

Boon: "It's just not often creatures have heads several kilometers long!"

"Well, he is not a creature," Ira said, "he is responsible for keeping our planet together along with his dying mother. And should Zorath succeed at his plan, we would all perish. Seranor as a planet would crumble." Ira paused to scan across the table and to look into each of their faces one-by-one. "So this is important."

"Can these devices, these Arvinstrum pieces, be used for other purposes? Can they in themselves be used as arvic weapons?" asked Alexan.

"Maybe Khan, can answer that," Ira turned to Khan who was surprised at Ira's gesture. How did he know about what Zorath did? He truly was gifted with knowledge and was probably why Khan liked him. In some ways, he was similar to his father but more militarily inclined which his father always stayed away from.

"I was unfortunate enough to have witnessed its destructive power. The device was called Seca, carver of the land, and when Seca was called to strike by the hand of Zorath himself she released an awful wave of flamma energy unlike I have yet to have seen again, and it struck Ulaq, the town I grew up, and it wiped it clean leaving only a giant hole where a lake has since formed. They named it, Lake Tulai, after my father, since it was he who was to be killed. Instead, all the thousands of innocent entans died and my father and I escaped."

The room went quiet. Ira handed back Khan's bastion whispering something in his ear. He told him that he knew he wouldn't kill the thief but did it to convince Boon that Khan was serious and determined. That was the main reason why Boon remained.

It was Alexan who broke the silence. "Ira, can these two devices be carried safely?"

"They are non-functional without knowing how to use them. So it will not require anything special," Ira said then went on to explain. "One item is a protective device, the other I'm not sure, it may be one of sealing or of cleansing. It does not matter. You are not to use them. They can cause great destruction to the land and to yourselves. The level of arvicity that passes through them can rearrange molecular structure because they were designed for use by the Kozotal."

"Where are they kept?" asked Alexan.

"In a sealed chamber that has not been opened for hundreds of tios," said the underground military leader. He was the crux of the Terium. His theories were made real. The four of them knew this.

"Then how will we enter?" asked Alexan, again.

"That is where our thief comes in," Ira began, pointed an outstretched finger at the secretive and self-preserving fellow. "You see, Boon is not just a thief though he wastes his time with petty things and throws his real talents to the shat hole: He is gifted with the ability to open locks and the creativity to remove the value kept inside. You would not tell of those skills by merely looking at him."

"It's luck," added Boon.

"Call it what you like," said Ira, "but he is required to get you all inside and to disarm the mechanical and other traps you might run into. And you, Alexan, must be able to dispel some of the embedded arvicity inside that will try to stop you. I will give you an arvic spell enhancer to help you but you must practice and increase your ability. The other two know their places well enough."

"Ira, we met something strange on our way here. It was why we were late," said Khan. Ira, if by chance he didn't know, should be told.

Alexan: "You mean the synthetic beings?"

Griz: "Their milk froze my armor."

Alexan: "And a bunch of other things such as my clothes. They have no respect for fashion."

Griz: "What are flacking about, Alexan?"

Alexan: "I'm not—"

Ira: "Tell me more!"

Khan recounted the story about the bluish white warriors, explaining in detail what had happened in the streets.

Ira: "Then he is already here." Ira rolled his eyes in search of information all the while rolling a new strategy to replace the old that had been in place.

Khan: "Who is here?"

Ira: "Denar'ka."

Khan: "Who?"

"A servant of Zorath who was once with the Terium," Ira replied, not willing to explain the story. "We must not detract ourselves too much. I will only tell you this. Those synthetic beings that you encountered are part of Zorath's army. They are called the Army of Naquior for their milk is made of naqui."

"That explains your armor, Griz," said Khan.

"We have yet to fully understand their capabilities," Ira started, "so if you meet them be careful. They are as merciless as is their king. They grow in numbers and prefer to remain in the colder regions but now they are here. Strange. I will look

into this further and know more upon your return."
His calm appearance gave no indication of what was
running through his cerbus. A hundred strategies
bolted this way and that. Some rejected entirely,
others pushed to the next stage of testing.
Strategies were in the process of reformulation.

"We'll need some weapons and armor if we are
going to find these ancient relics and live to tell
about it," said Khan.

Griz agreed. "Weapons and armor."

"I have prepared some for you." Ira's servant
walked in with two medium-sized packs, one black
and one white. He reached inside to reveal some
items. "Alexan, this ring and bracelet are both arvic
enhancers. The ring stores arvicity which you can
draw upon when casting. It also enables you to cast
more powerful spells with very low chances of
failure. The bracelet identifies and dispels both
items and spells." Spells, the manipulation of
arvicity, were accessible to all students. But those
who tried to cast spells of a higher complexity than
they were capable of managing often faced failure
and, sometimes, death. The arvicerer Raknor came
to cerbind. The ring would allow Alexan to act as if
he were of greater power than he really was. "And
this last ring here is what you will need to locate the
entrance," Alexan said as he opened his palm
revealing a crystal ring in the center. "When you
reach the spot on the map you will call the command
that I will teach you before you leave and the portal
to let you in will be shown to you. Otherwise, there
is no way in." Alexan grabbed it but before he could

pull it away Ira grabbed his wrist. He said very slowly to the new party member: "Do not lose it. This ring took a lot of effort to make."

Next, Ira took out a small box and a pair of glasses. He said: "These glasses, which fit over the ears, give you, Boon, nightvision and allows you to see objects invisible in nature. They also help to translate difficult elos and protect your eyes from things that might damage them. This box contains a higher quality thieve's kit than yours including this grappling hook that sticks to any surface, and a fine but dense rope with which to climb. It carries a maximum of two bodies at one time."

Another servant had come in with a batier in a scabbard and a small box. Ira whispered something in the servant's ear and he rushed out. "Khan, this is your new batier. It's called Radiant and cuts through hard materials easily. When unsheathed the rod heats enough to melt skin and armor. Give me your bastion." Khan did so, reluctantly. "Don't break it! In this box is a vial of strength, many healing potions and a special tard. The tard is 99.9% secure and traceable by me. It can also send data and images through our new flamma net."

The servant returned with a soft suit of clothing, gray in color, with a hood at the top. "Griz, this is for you."

"I'm not one of those kind of lutos," replied Griz.

"This is your new armor," said Ira.

"That's no armor, Ira. That's a dancing suit and I don't dance," said Griz, angry at the unexpected insult. "Why don't you give it to the fashion designer over there." Griz shook his head toward Alexan.

"Are you calling me a fashion designer, you oblong cora root?" replied Alexan.

"Stop!" interjected Ira. "Time is very valuable. Why is it that the lot of you just can't stop arguing?"

"Maybe, and it's just me talking here, we're not a 'lot'," said Boon.

"You and the rest of you better get it right. And if I find out that the mission fails because of your differences then I will ensure that you will never sleep soundly again. Am I clear on this?" Ira said. Short nods came one at a time.

"Ira, I'm not going to wear a suit," said Griz. "I choose armor and nothing more."

"I know. I've had it in storage for some time. I don't know why you shouldn't have it," Ira said, tossing the suit to the brutal fighter. "It changes to hardened lutium plate armor, at will. This armor is also self-cleaning and regenerates damage done to it. Try it on."

Griz removed the few pieces of armor left except his black girdle. That he did not touch. Then, with his back to his friends he removed his helm and put on the suit. In an instant the suit transformed into beautiful gray lutium full plate armor.

"That's some suit!" said Boon.

"That's Griz's new armor!" said Griz. He walked around in it.

"I thought that you'd like it. Okay, list down any other equipment that you need and I will furnish

what is reasonable," said Ira then proceeded to
leave.

"Wait. We forgot one important thing – zorn,"
said Boon.

"With all the recent events I have lost the
perspective of wealth. But yes, surely I promised
you zorn. How much do you want, Boon?"

"Ten thousand zorn plus the items we find outside
of the directives."

"Is that reasonable to you all?" asked Ira to
everyone.

"Wait one minute, I think that we should get paid
a base amount then a bonus for the work that is
successful," said Khan.

"Tell me your thoughts – quick," said Ira.

"It is of certain danger and of unknown danger.
What guards the last two pieces of the Arvinstrum
will not be a bunch of guards with batiers. I
appreciate the thieve's simple salary but truly this
mission can be our end," explained the young wind
master.

"Or your beginning. All the arvic items you find
you can keep. Any treasure you find is yours. That
may prove more wealthy than your pay and I will
furnish the whole expedition. Do not be so
voracious, Khan."

"I want a base 20,000 zorn for each of us and a
bonus 20,000 for each piece that is brought back
intact."

"I'll go with that," Boon said quickly changing his
position.

"Do the rest of you agree? After this there is no further bargaining."

Two nods came from Griz and Alexan.

"Done!" said Ira.

Chapter 13

NATA AND Niva were the spirits of interaction. Nata breathed freedom and carved unimpeded paths as its airy touch gently guided those wishing to be led. And while Nata freely enchanted life, it was Niva who worked to contain, to preserve bodies, ideas, and pieces of matter and antimatter. He apathetically repressed life in cold material crafted from his frosty palms. As Nata soared, Niva succumbed to his own icy restraints, and in that containment a fresh authority was born: ice. The ice was the pure, a rawness filtered by process and procedure, and to be able to wield such contained purity was considered to make the mortal, immortal; the free, subdued; the lost, found.

Followers of Niva, like the Equists of wind, could gain the attributes of ice, and, in doing so, all of his abilities. There had been a dedicated group of followers that followed him and respected his pureness. The masters of ice, Nivatons, learned to transform their body into iceform. It was an awesome form because of its dichotomy. The splicing of ice with living ceramic tissue shifted the innate solid properties into a supple, dense material. Strikes in iceform were deadly. They broke their targets; armor and weapons cracked when limbs of ice hit.

The highest level of iceform was that of the naqui iceform, an entire body of scorching liquid ice, what Nivatons referred to as reaching the *arkti state*. In arkti, a master disciple's body shifted and flexed easily as a unit of living naqui, and when any contact was made, their opponent's body froze instantly in the area that was struck. Vital strikes to the head or chest automatically stopped the internal bodily functions and the opponent died clutching their frozen organs. A Nivaton in arkti was difficult to kill. Damage done to their body was instantly repaired by circulating naqui that reconstructed itself when and where needed. The naqui molecules, packed tightly as porcelan, were inseparable and at the same time pliable. A suit of armor, a deadly weapon and the intellect to drive them all combined together as one entity.

Arkti could not be maintained for long at risk of losing control of the naqui form and having it spread outward killing the disciple instantly. It was a volatile state kept together by a handful of atoms on the fringe of death. While in arkti, disciples could also increase abilities and heal prior damage among other things, though few have lived to say more than that. The greatest master was T-Non, a ventan who achieved arkti at the young age of fifty. It was he who found Denar'ka, a hundred tios later, as a young luto crying in the street. After hearing his story about a wind master who refused to train him, he decided to take him as a student.

Shifting to arkti was extremely hazardous and many masters have lost limbs for attempting this. The real test was immersing oneself in pure naqui. E-Non, full name Denar'ka-e-Non, was a gifted young Nivaton working alongside Ira Levin, but the day since he was taken by Kalorian-Sint in the Ice Scabbard, and changed sides, his iceform abilities have increased five multiples. In his enhanced arkti training he lost both his feet and his entire right forearm but has lived and became the most powerful Nivaton on Seranor after killing T-Non in a duel that left his former teacher in three frozen chunks.

He could maintain the arkti state for as long as he chose. E-Non was no longer his name but insisted that his disciples all adopt such names, in some way to respect his first teacher. His closest disciple was V-Non who had achieved arkti state under his close supervision.

Like many of the elemental professions, Nivatons must practice in order to refine their skills. Denar'ka was often found waist deep in naqui in his chosen training spot. Immersion in naqui while in arkti state enabled him to reach new levels of iceform increasing not only his mastery but the density of his body, freezing level of naqui form, and the regenerative powers though this last set of abilities still could not help him to replace his feet because at the time of losing them he damaged the porcelan flesh and scarred himself permanently. It was his reminder. Playing in naqui while in arkti gave him the most joy and took him away from the deeds of the day. Zorath had led him on a new path, one that encouraged him to redevelop himself to a point of superiority. There was nothing to stop the influence from the Nivian King, it oozed from his lips and poured out in his voice striking all that was able to hear it.

Smartness was matched with gruesomeness. Toleration was not Denar'ka's talent and he did not hesitate to strike down those that exceeded his patience. Most often he struck the head with an extended naqui arm that left behind an iced head that splintered into tiny shards when it hit the ground. He had tortured some of Ira's crew to obtain information and retrieved it by freezing the hands of the captives and then crushing their fingers one-by-one as they watched. Most entans made it through losing three fingers, two actually managed to watch both of their forearms be crunched before surrendering all that they knew. Of course, they were later sent into the naqui to die but not before removing the cerbus so that it could be studied and perhaps later used. Denar'ka had always been aggressive in his ways, and the longer he studied arkti, his psychoses became inflamed and his mental capacity unfolded a few steps more. He termed it, "the highest intelligence achievable by an entan". Zorath remained his mentor as his knowledge of ice was by far the greatest and the Nivian's milk was pure naqui. A dream Denar'ka once had.

Something more occupied the cerbind of Denar'ka. Just before the disappearance of the wind Equists and the arrival of the Sints, he had arranged to meet Equist Nao for a battle of wind versus ice. An old match: overdue.

The image of Nao burned in the back of his eyes and steam clouded his cerbind. Nothing had gone wrong as a seedling. In all respects, Denar'ka grew up in an average life of comfort, stability and leniency provided by his parents in the urba of Storh. Life in the urba was peaceful and his father, Ujar-e-non, was a sculptor. His overweight mother, Candil-e-non, served on several local committees dedicated to keeping the environment free of waste and pollution. Every six months the residents of Storh held an ice-sculpture competition. Ujar was a reigning champion well-respected in the community and given precedence to how he lived his life. A comfortable residence was given to him on one particular tio after Ujar sculpted a long, shimmering snake. What stood out, and the reason why he won the competition, was because the scales of the snake, each of the more than one thousand carefully hand-carved, were colorized by a method that no one else knew. He did not even share it with his seedling, Denar'ka. It solidified his position as a true expert in the art of sculpting and Ujar decided to retire that day so that he could teach his one seedling how to be as great as he was.

Many of the other sculptors, including Qua Li-Grum, were not happy with his decision to retire. They had yet beaten him in competition and were not going to accept his retirement before they had taken advantage of his high record. Ujar did not care nor listen and retired. Qua's seedling, Nao, didn't care what his father did. He spent most of his time beating up or finding ways to terrorize little Denar'ka. Nao wasn't big at all. In fact, his stature was small compared to most of the seedlings but he was aggressive and sometimes violent in his methods. His parents could not even control him and he usually got what he wanted from other seedlings as well.

Denar'ka could not taste any beauty in ice nor in most things. Nao's beatings subtracted from the remaining ounces of joy in his life. The cold ice ached in his body, drawing ambition further away from his corius. His father, so hopelessly devoted to his family, didn't listen, wouldn't listen and forced Denar'ka to learn the art which had given him status and responsibility in the positions of life. Positions were the footsteps of adulthood.

The two of them would take regular trips to the westernmost region at the Rim of Nival, the highest mountain range on Seranor and the place from which severe cold originated. Kyata Lake, the source of the best ice for sculpting because of its dense fibers and cold-keeping ability, about three hours walk from Storh, was found. It was told that Kyata Lake was fed by the kium-laced aqua from the central mountains. Kium, black ice, was unbreakable and continued to emit cooling properties for indefinite periods though could be handled by a bare hand without any problem. Denar'ka dug and sawed chunks of ice from the lake with his father, and then was required to haul the formless pieces back to the urba where they could work on them. When the weather was too hot, the two of them lived by the lake for several weeks as the practiced the art of ice sculpting. Denar'ka hated every minute of every day during those times and dreamed of one day escaping his father's persecutive love.

It was at that time, about his eightieth tio, that Denar'ka began to listen to the stories of Pri-im and the wind Equists. Those that worshipped Nata were the free and Denar'ka wanted her power. After he heard that Nao left to join Pri-im in Canyon D'Altu, he too wanted to go but his father refused. Anger rose in him for the first time in his life. That anger soon metamorphosed into rage, then to violence and finally to derangement. It was derangement that capsulated him and forced Denar'ka to drown his father in Kyata Lake, leaving him to die as a sculpture. The memory of his frozen father haunts him still.

When he arrived at the Canyon, Nao had already been accepted and had learned many of the basic skills known to the Equists. Nao was liked by Pri·im and studied under him directly. And he was different too, calmer than before as if an oratic device had been plucked from his cerbind. It angered Denar'ka to see the one who was so violent to him now accepted as a student of pacifism. Ironic. And displeasing. Pri·im and the others would not accept Denar'ka. And two tios later, when he was finally let into the circle, Denar'ka could not learn any longer. His corius was filled with hate that blocked Nata's love. The young luto was whisked away by a powerful wind after his rage erupted and he attacked Nao. Even then, Nao Li·Grum could defend himself using the wind strike and this removed half of Denar'ka's left ear.

ZOLDIER PRODUCTION was at a maximum and Zorath wanted it improved further to achieve his mission to create the Army of Naquior, synthetic beings designed to enter Nivata and to strike down all those who betrayed him and cast him out. To achieve this end was going to require Seranor's support, with or without her permission. She had already provided him with the raw materials, soon she would help him to open the gate from one world to the next.

Denar'ka satisfied the needs of his new king with the unique knowledge he obtained while under the command of Ira Levin. This proved more than useful to Zorath as he was later able to predict Ira's moves more easily based on previous patterns of intelligence and strategies. Even Kozotian cerbinds could be cracked if their patterns could be established. That was the one key to Zorath's advantage on this planet. A mathematical and scientific cerbind, at a level progressively beyond genius, could find patterns in all things. Patterns determined possibilities which were then used to determine action. Counter action was completely effective against a well known and understood future action. With Denar'ka's help, and that of others, Zorath and his Sints moved steps ahead of Seranor though for an unknown reason Ira was still able to elude.

Talk of Equists distracted Denar'ka more than he realized and was not aware that Kalia-Sint and Kalier-Sint had arrived. Official business for the king. All business related to Zorath was official. The armed and potent Sint crusaders were both the hand and voice of the king with the ability to indulge his demands as was needed.

"You have come early as always," said Denar'ka, not happy at their presence. As much as he worshipped ice, he did not trust the artificial crusaders. They accepted his disrespect. Denar'ka was an important player in the hierarchy, that much they understood. But importance was not fixed and while he had a position of authority, the Nivaton would surely take advantage of it. "We will prepare. Any news?"

"Levin has prepared," said Kalia-Sint.

"If not for my contact we would not have come this far," replied Denar'ka. "Imagine where we would be then."

"Enough talk of your connections. The king has made his commands and they will be served. There is nothing more to add," she replied.

"It is my strategy and plan that succeeded last, as it will succeed now. Remember Sint, you answer to me," said Denar'ka.

"Certainly, Nivaton Denar'ka. As long as you follow our king's directives and keep your successes."

"There is one upon them called Khan. He is a wind follower. I will test this young wind follower before taking our goods and slaughtering them."

"As you wish, Nivaton."

Over the next half an hour, Denar'ka and his synthetic squad arranged for their immediate travel. The capture of the two Arvinstrum pieces, Septana and Lavo, would complete the collection of the seven Arvinstrum pieces, the tools that would extract Seragorn. Before that could happen, the artus locks had to be found and they were proving difficult even for Zorath.

The upper lake was completely frozen and rays of colorful flamma filtered down onto the underground Battlekeep Vatu. An immensely large cavern had been carved out of the mountain, under the lake, and an ice Battlekeep was fitted in the center of a second lake, this one made of naqui.

As the bunch of them stood atop the main deck, beautiful streams of light, coming from the expansive ceiling of ice, filtered down and was reflected in a little white box. The same box taken from Khan not long before. Pyx kept Denar'ka's hand warm, but his face was unsettled. Pyx was unopened. His smartest cerborian arvicians were unable to open it, and his hypothesis: Should the ordinary Shev'la Khan be capable of opening such a straightforward ceramic package then so should he, the most intelligent entan on the planet; was unresolved.

"Maintain your places," Denar'ka said to Kalia-Sint. The grotesque reflection of his own face stared back from her visor. He felt the pain of disgust to see his horrid, hairless head. The sight of his left ear caused him to fixate. The investment he made. He blamed his sacrifice on Nao, and with Nao gone, probably recirculated in Nata's bowels, it was Khan who remained to fire his ambition, and he detested Khan for having been able to open the first two shells of this mysterious white package in his hand. Only Zorath would know of what it could do. Denar'ka's loathing for his seedhood foe naturally moved onto Nao's protégé, and though the thought of meeting Khan face-to-face excited him, he was not removed from his service to the overall plan. "The future of this package, I will leave here."

"Our efforts are insufficient as they stand," she said. "Deal with the box after."

"They are sufficient," Denar'ka had already walking part of the way to the open portal. He turned around and said: "We will be in time to catch when they come and not when they go in. Wouldn't

you rather let them do the work first?" He entered
the building.

Kalia and Kalier, along with a score of zoldiers,
stood frigidly erect near the flashport device.

Chapter 14

THERE WAS a cosmic, icy beauty about Battlekeep Vatu, Denar'ka's cryptic operations at the northern tip of Aqua Ora, eighteen kilometers into the snow-capped mountains above Maffin. Zorath constructed the kium-black underground keep after abandoning Ghon and needed a new home while he made plans for his great keep in the Mountains of Nival, known as the Ice Rim.

The rod of Seca along with his unearthly arvic skills enabled him to release just the right amount of flamma to shape the ice as he so desired and a massive Battlekeep was erected under a great ice lake. Large production devices were constructed and implanted in the lower levels of the tall Keep shortly after Vatu was carved. With his new base of operations headquartered deep within the coldest region of the Ice Rim, the Nivian left his new commander, Denar'ka‑e‑non, having recently completed his arkti training, in charge.

Denar'ka had spent a majority of his time here preparing the most complex project he had ever had been given, and only on occasion left the Vatu to manage the unpredictable, but necessary, variables that bobbed up from time to time on the outside. Entans, even those deformed and psychotic, proved to be much more sympathetic than any of the Sint crusaders. Strategic actions necessitated workable relationships, so strategic partnerships were put in place and, for the short term, were relied upon. The Nivaton walked through Vatu like the captain of a ship who knew every square meter of his vessel as he knew the palm of his hand. Familiar signals were given, commands whispered and guards passed by without any slowing down.

The milky cold temperatures did not even bother him. A normal entan entering this place would have been frozen dead – milk frappe – within the first two minutes, assuming that they survived the thousands of meters high climb to actually get here, in the middle of a tall mountain; and were able to circumambulate the trained guards on every corner, and after all of that, were able to disarm the traps and avoid the detection devices that automatically alerted another detachment of guards. Vatu was partially alive with the characteristics of a colossal zoldier.

The upper-levels, situated on the topside, housed the morb and cerborian servants and guards. In the first and second level basement were storage rooms for food, weapons and production equipment. A few levels down, riding on the arvic lift at the center of a gargantuan hall, Denar'ka reached his private and executive rooms and, beneath that, the production areas. At the very bottom were two cylindrical portals, one on each side, used to access the CHAMBER OF CONTROLLED EXPERIMENTS (CCE). New zoldiers and weapons were always in development.

Synthetic naqui zoldiers, or just zoldiers, bluish-white skinned with white eyes, were first produced from the second month. The first batch, Zoldier, did not live as long as Zorath expected nor had near the amount of attributes that he wanted. By Zoldier Series 3 (third version in the series), using crystalloids, arvic-laced crystals found deep in Nivata Lake, he was able to enhance the bodies of the S3s with vivotic ice, activated ice with arvic conductivity, and a kium-laced skeleton that was near impossible to sever. He also added coolvision eyes so that they could see all things in variants of flammic exposure or emmitance, and softened the ice on the face so that it could masticate simple verse for basic communications.

To keep the energy flowing to all parts of the body, he invented synthetic entan milk and spliced these atoms together with those of naqui creating an energy transfer medium that also burned if exposed to the outside. But the most perfect of all wasn't that the zoldiers had an innate healing ability enhanced in cold areas, no, that wasn't the most sublime, it was the fact that when truly finished the zoldier's body would turn to aqua leaving nothing for the enemy to touch, take or trust. Even the kium-laced skeleton was designed to dissolve once the body had perished. The naqui zoldiers were originally created to stroke his giant ego, but as new technological developments surfaced, he took advantage of them and modified his synthetic creations. He perfected them. From this, the Zoldier S3 was formed.

When Zorath left Vatu, he put in charge hundreds of morb and scores of cerbors to run the Battlekeep. They all wore ice bracelets to protect them from extended stays in the deadly frigid temperatures. Denar'ka was commander-in-chief. He had earned his place by Ira's side and when he had survived the transformation into arkti state, under Zorath's guidance, he earned his promotion.

The factories were now producing just under 700 zoldiers a day in addition to their ice armor and weapons, special items were given to select zoldiers whose attributes were more succinct and superior to the standard.

The first and second series of zoldiers have long since become aqua. The third generation of naqui zoldiers were stable enough and have been embedded with natural fighting skills steps ahead of the Seronian Guard. A fourth model zoldier has been in development for some time but not finalized. Zorath has been preoccupied with the resilience and tenacity of the resistant Terium and was not able to harmonize high amounts of arvicity into the synthetic bodies without destroying the physical shape. When finished, the S4s will form a special military unit with possible mass production at a future date. An army of S4s would dominate the planet.

Production has a sterilized quietness about it deep inside the keep. Naqui was pumped from the wide naqui lake surrounding the lower levels. The naqui was then combined with synthetic milk and stored in large cylindrical containers of strengthened ice. Here it would be whipped into a 50:50 blend and injected with a mild dose of liquefied arvicity.

The bodies were formed from a porcelan-ice mixture that was poured into an entan-like mold and heated by a low level flamma over several hours. Once completed into a pliable shell it was fitted onto a skeleton then filled by soft ice. Once the naqui milk was run through for three days, the head was implanted with an arvic ball, the size of an entan's fist, and this then connected the zoldier to the seamless photon network with which they communicated.

The distributed photon net was commanded and presided over by Kozo, Zorath's assistant, from a secret station in the Ice Rim, and could send information both ways, at will. The station housed the main flammascope, an integral and powerful communication device solely used for zoldier manipulation. A massive dish containing tens of thousands of tiny crystals, multi-colored, managed all ranges of communications. A secondary flammascope was situated at Vatu.

All Zorath's demands were passed through the net to guide the zoldiers. Pertinent information was downloaded into a flamma sphere that could be accessed as the Nivian so needed. His knowledge became the combined knowledge of all. The addition of zoldiers multiplied the accumulated information and threatened the contained knowledge of leading Seronians, and even the Kozoty.

Currently, the one thing that still eluded Zorath was when, in the absence of cold, the zoldiers could not exist. He had experimented with potions of naqui essence to temporarily correct this weakness though it was not available in a large enough quantity as was needed to support a full scale army over a period of time. This setback had forced the zoldiers to remain in the colder regions and was why all of them were shipped to the mountainous area near the base station.

Doubly productive was his freezing of the planet's core. Zorath had captured an ice malkar and using an advanced power magnifier he fed the malkar's power into the planet. Degree by degree, the planet was getting colder and as the realm of wintry cold grew so too did the area in which the zoldiers could roam freely.

Once fully completed the zoldiers were transported through a large flashport that Zorath encrypted and secured. Zoldiers were flashed to an identical flashport hidden in the mountains, deep underground, and awaited their need for activation in large storage rooms.

Denar'ka reached his trusty cerborian servant, Crispier. He was given the name because his skin and natural armor was blacker than usual. This anomaly earned him distinction at the keep, and he was resilient in battle as well as handy with arvic spells.

Crispier acknowledged Denar'ka and immediately followed him into a private cell. There he handed Crispier the white package. The secret box that had not been opened. Pyx was as clean and as perfect as when she was first unveiled in Khan's residence.

Crispier glanced at his hand, spoke a few words and moments later three cerbors entered the room. The box sat innocently on the empty table.

"This box must be opened before I return," Denar'ka started. "Study it well and make your predictions accurate. It is more ancient than it appears and made by a Kozotal. This much is true. But I want to see what is inside this box and the three of you will open or one of – and I don't care which one – will die. You will choose who that is. I only want this box open and the contents revealed to me upon my return. You have two days."

Crispier swung his eyes over his three best researchers, masters of knowledge, arvicity, and technology before he responded to Denar'ka. "It will be open as you have asked," said Crispier, confident in tone. Satisfied, the commander-in-chief returned to his cell to retrieve something and then went topside. The Sints had waited an hour. There was no remark to his tardiness.

The deathly black Vatu, derived from a heavy concentration of kium, was centralized in a large cavern several kilometers underneath the planet's elevated surface directly underneath a lake of solid ice, two kilometers thick. A large corridor was burrowed opposing the front gate and eventually led to the outside but none really knew how long it was. A black bridge connected the corridor with the keep.

As he reached the waiting Sints, his first disciple, V-Non, had returned along with the two others. Their rigid fists signaled in greeting and after Denar'ka left.

AMONG OTHER things, V-Non was setting up a chain of ice form training schools, called the IceFist, in three of the major urbas including Casus. Two external camps trained the higher level IceFist disciples while Vatu was reserved for only the most adept like V-Non and a couple others. Denar'ka still wanted his own non-synthetic group of followers and was why he planned to use the IceFist schools to indoctrinate and train entans in the ways of the ice form, the ultimate combat style.

Wind training had largely disappeared in the urbas. Most, if any, took place in the canyons or the plains where the wind was highest and Nata, the most abundant. Wind followers, especially the no-name Equists, were the wanderers of the land. They

were the loveless and the blissful. When the nine
Equists returned to Nata, Khan was the surviving
sign of a soon-to-be extinct ideology that promised
peace and accountability. Nata was the balancer of
life on the planet and her fingers and arms had been
retracted.

It wasn't at all odd that Khan both realized and
didn't react to this very fact: He was the only
existing Equist, as far as anyone knew, left on
Seranor. At least in physical form. But the
unpredictable Khan, who kept his name, did not
consider himself to be an Equist. He had failed to
achieve the state of windstorm among the other
skills that Nao and his nameless brothers had shown
him.

There were times that Khan toyed with the idea
of running schools to teach entans the beauty and
the insanity of Nata. He could never get past the
idea of it. The conclusion that insanity was not for
everyone prevented him from exploring the concept.
Again, he was blocked by his intellect. If he could
only let go of his predictive ideas it might help him
to realize his potential. And the other excuse, he
liked this one much better, was that he was still a
seedling trapped in a luto's body. He still wanted to
taste the adventure and to be free to choose the same
as all young are free to do and choose what they
want to do. He was refusing to extend his identity.
That was basically it. Schools meant responsibility
for others. Khan had problems with the
responsibility for himself and his rag-tag team of
mercenary adventurers. Why they even considered

staying together, he didn't understand. Griz, Alexan and Boon were diametrically opposed in practically all of their thinking and ways of execution. And, he himself, could only see as far as the goal in his cerbind. Leading the bunch of them forward into the unknown; the nothing and the everything.

A thief in his party would make breaking into structures easier by a magnitude and, similarly, would open the vein of distrust among them. Thieves only knew about one rule: protect the self above and beyond all else. He would be taking a big risk to keep this thief in his party, but under Ira's orders he had no choice. Khan trusted Ira and if Ira had recommended Boon, then Boon it would be. He could trust Griz. Could he trust Alexan? A Kozoty from the north, born and bred in luxury, may not have the persistence necessary to remain as a wild adventurer, living days in complete obscurity and on the verge of life and death.

Life and death still thrilled Khan. His family, once living, was now all dead. And those who hadn't died had left, leaving the same mark on his corius. So he only cared about life. High risk, bodily pain, milk loss and absolute fear reminded him of life. Reminded him of what he was because sometimes it was difficult to remember what he was and all that he remembered was what he had lost. Why was he kept alive? Death should have become of him, but it didn't. Nexa didn't find him for some reason. The pain of it all, of losing what was closest to him, burned the milk running through his body, and set it aflame. Without adventure he would consume

himself in his lust to find nexa. Without adventure
he was a symbiosis. A shell filled with a misplaced
kol.

The higher the risk and greater the peril, the
more interested he became. Working with Ira gave
him some predictability and preparedness but the
real chase, the real taste of what life was remained
in the unprepared adventures where danger was
around the simplest corner and a constant aching
was their reminder. It may have been that Khan
wanted to die, or at least to see how far he could
push his physical, mental, and emotional limits
before he died. To see if he could achieve all that he
was made to be. And realistically speaking, if that
were possible with the enigma of Shev'la Khan, he
wanted to know if it was all worth the pain of
existence. That was the only thing in his cerbind.

To exist was to know pain.

To push forward was to soothe the grief and
sorrow inside.

Interaction. The more he interacted with the
environment, the more alive he felt and the stronger
he became, and if reality didn't someday kill him, he
would achieve what he really was made to finish. As
the ancient philosopher Xan used to say, "Purpose is
syncategorematic."

In his training and in his dreams, he sometimes
met Equist Nao. He was grayish and wasted. It
bothered him to see Nao like that. It bothered him
now and not so much before. Khan continued to
train on a daily basis. There were days of extreme

intensity and days of calm. He fought within himself the rights and the wrongs.

Without a proper teacher, he felt lost at times. His moves were unrefined and exotic to the ways of the old. In his corius, he knew his wind forms to be fundamentally correct and effective. He had confirmed this in battle. It was the lack of trust in his own methods which discouraged more than it should have. Khan felt like he was betraying Nao from his unorthodox ways, even if they were effectual. There was no choice but to continue and each hour of training enabled him to excel that much more. He forgot about the fact that he was the last possible Equist and, once in a while, juggled the idea that he could open up his own training schools. Teach Seronians a better way to defend themselves and to win their confidence in melee.

Teach them a peaceful way of life.

It was early. He knew it without knowing.

Too early to consider settling down. Instead it was time for risk.

Time for adventure.

Time for living.

Time to be.

Chapter 15

FOUR HEAVILY loaded and commissioned
adventurers rode at the top of a string of hills,
silhouetted against a sky-blue backdrop filled with
tiny specs of falling rain. Packed talins, new clothes,
clean faces, and polished weapons highlighted the
strangers in nature's palm. Cora was perfect for all
types of weather and aqua beaded off of their clothes
and equipment, back safely into the earthy ground to
nourish the mother. Their white skin glistened in
the wet of the rain save Griz's ugly face that was
masked under his new grayish plate armor. He
heard the pitter-patter of rain drops on his helm,
and the armor sparkled just the same.

Day after day, the wet weather beat down on them and slow progression became the safest and surest way to get to their destination. Talin travel was a tedium that many endured and did not like. Talins never tired like entans and other beings, and they were at the mercy of the planet's arvic flows. Turbulent, dry or dark pools of arvicity changed courses of travel and riders had no choice but to accept it or walk by foot. A talin could be forced to ride onto such diverse sources of energy, and it would certainly seal their death and dissipation. Many trips became unpredictable. Time was difficult to measure and when it was measured, the travelers could better prepare for the ordeal. Excess time was used for reflection. Most adventuring types were generally too excited when moving into risk, rather than surviving it and returning home, to think.

The foursome continued. The path wound along a string of hills that stretched for more than ten kilometers in all directions. The special tard device given by Ira emitted a detailed map onto a small flammic screen. The grassy green area they were in was labeled as HILL PARK but Griz liked to call it the Green Bosom. It kept a smile on his face and the others could tell because of his occasional short bouts of chuckling. They passed an occasional tall tree, spaced apart relatively uniformly with a wide trunk at the bottom, sitting atop a hill, and used it as a marker.

Even the Green Bosom couldn't prevent Griz's boredom from slipping by, followed by Boon's strong distaste for outer-urba travel, three days later. The new addition to the party enjoyed the outdoors, breathing deeply its fertile stench. For some reason, ideas such as boredom and monotony didn't get Khan stirred. He was far happier to be alive than to concern himself with what he phrased as "distracting one's energy rather than harvesting it". Khan kept in contact with Ira by using the tard. It was the only tard they brought with them since it was the only one that would work this far from a major urba. Three short calls – even Ira didn't take unnecessary security risks – a day were made.

Tension grew in Ira's voice but not his face. The voice was always the first to reveal the imbalance inside, and if the voice wrestled, the tension only became more evident. Ira knew this and it made difficult for Khan to discern the real amount of his usually dead calm friend.

The four party members traveled together without speaking more than one or two whole sentences each. They all marched on regardless. What they did share in common was the yearning for action. An itch to fight spread amongst them. An itch in their milk.

After the seventh day the weather ceased sprinkling rain and it became a stale blue all over. A cool breeze flowed over the low hills they traveled on. Khan decided to take a rest at the next tree. He had been counting them. Every thirty trees they rested and it was time for another break. Today, Ira had been very curt in his communication. In half an hour, all but one was pleasantly napping: Griz stood

on guard, too restless to sleep. It might have been
the withdrawal from anaprimo that kept his system
so stimulated. He had had trouble sleeping since
day-one.

While keeping guard, he heard a muffled noise, a
rumbling, that came in wave-like pitches, and was
not willing to remove his helm to hear it more
clearly. He never took off his helm not even during
sex with Number 51. And didn't care now for some
little noise. Danger? Not possible. How dangerous
could it be in the Green Bosom? Nothing was seen
for as far as his eye could see.

The longer the sound stayed around, the surer he
was that it wasn't coming from the air. He touched
his breastplate and the sound became even more
muffled then he released it and heard the low
rumbling more clearly. His armor plates were
faintly humming. It wasn't a sound at all. His
armor was vibrating, and the vibration was coming
from the ground. The ground shook lightly and
resonated until it massaged the top of his helm.

Alexan was the first to wake and was intently
pointing his ear to the ground when Khan rose.
Alexan heard the whirling scream, but to Khan's
untrained ear there was only the physical vibration
which by now had increased in intensity.

"What is it, Alexan?" Khan asked.

"There is something in the ground," said Alexan.
He jerked his head left then right as if tuning in to
the sound. "It is going in all directions." He listened
further then stopped. "Seranor...something is in
pain."

"What pain? What is happening?" said Khan.

"It screams in pain and there is anger. We must get up. Boon, wake!" yelled Alexan.

Boon stirred, opened his eye to check, then seeing nothing closed it again.

"Up!" said Khan, kicking the thieve's foot hard.

"Ouch! That hurt. I'm going to ask for more zorn if you do that again for no reason," Boon said, his eyes were still closed. "There is nothing there," he added.

"You don't get out much, do you?" said Alexan as he anxiously got up. "Prepare our talins. We must get ready to move. It comes closer."

"What is it?" asked Khan, not satisfied with the information.

"It has the movement of a serpent but larger—" Alexan began.

"A serpent!" Boon screamed as he jumped up onto two feet. "Why didn't you tell me?"

"It's angry," said Alexan. "It is in rage and we are in danger."

The four mounted their talins and started riding away from the sound as per Alexan's sporadic instructions. Several hundred meters later, the sound all together stopped.

"Something is wrong. I have lost it," said Alexan. He shifted his head around trying to pick up its location. Nothing to confirm.

"Lost the serpent?" repeated Boon.

"Giant serpent," added Alexan.

"Great! You've just misplaced a short river," said Boon.

"Look who talks. You couldn't hear a morb shat if your back was turned and you were sitting beside him," said Griz, laughing to his own funny joke.

"Your hilarious, helmhead. You probably wear that helm because your afraid to see your dick," returned Boon.

"Quiet," said Alexan. "The sound comes again, but…"

Griz: "At least I have a dick." He laughed.

Boon: "Having a dick the size of a nod is not considered a dick."

Griz: "Having a clavus in your chest is considered to be dead."

Alexan: "Quiet! It comes closer…"

Boon: "If a clavus can actually get into my chest, I would be surprised."

Griz rotated his clavus. "Get ready for a BIG surprise."

Alexan: "I found it!"

Khan: "Where is it?"

Alexan: "Its…its right underneath us…"

"Run!" yelled the four of them in unison.

The talins bolted so fast that two of the riders were dropped where they were last. Only Khan and Alexan managed to stay on. Boon rolled away to the side. Griz was left semi-stunned, winded, from the drop in his heavy armor.

The ground shook violently then the hard clay fell inside a large hole. Khan threw a rope to Griz who caught on and tied it to his left wrist while holding onto his clavus with his one free hand. A large hole ten meters across opened and if it hadn't been for the rope would have swallowed Griz. Boon ran over to assist, then they both ran for cover together. Griz's encumbered pace slowed Boon down tremendously.

What looked like a smaller hill, reddish in color, emerged from the hole but when Alexan yelled "Serpent!" they all knew that it wasn't a hill. The gargantuan snake emerged in full, one hundred meters long and wide as a medium-sized ship. It roared in pain for what had been done to its land. It was angry.

Boon kept running and managed to get some distance between him and the hole. Griz, realizing that he wasn't getting anywhere uphill, stopped and turned to face the serpent forgetting to remove the rope still tied to his wrist. The serpent came barreling towards him at full speed. He grasped his two handed clavus tightly, then decided to charge it also. Khan ran into the fray seeing this as well as Alexan who prepared his spells.

Griz charged in and at the last point before hitting, dropped to one knee holding the clavus as tightly as possible with his supernatural grip, as it's underbody tried to smother him. The firmly placed clavus penetrated and ripped a long wound in the serpent's belly as its mass rolled over. Griz was finally squashed into the ground by the shear force of its tremendously large body and knocked unconscious still holding onto his clavus with both hands.

Khan whirled into the air and leapt onto the back of the beast. Two oxy bolts seared its oval head but only one penetrated the thick hide. Khan jumped

onto the slimy beast and danced on its scales as he
tried to find his balance. Finally he couldn't keep his
balance and so drove his batier deep inside its body.
The serpent kept moving. Boon had found a safe
spot behind a tree on a distance hill, but as the
serpent came roaring past, it swung its tail and
threw him and the tree flying into unconsciousness.
Khan stabbed and Alexan fired his flammic missiles
while the damage to its belly took its toll. Reddish
milk poured out of its fresh wounds. Without
warning, it dove again into the ground. Khan
floated off as he neared the ground and landed
safely.

"Griz! Boon! Griz! Boon! Where are you?" yelled
Khan. No response. He looked over to Alexan. "It's
gone."

"For now. I have never seen such anger in it
before," said Alexan.

"Something has disturbed it."

Minutes later all was quiet and Griz and Boon
both were regaining consciousness but had not fully
recovered when the ground violently shook again.

"Take cover!" yelled Khan. "Prepare your spells."

This time, the ground erupted and straight up it
went, straight as a long spike until it reached its full
height twelve stories high. Its milk poured from its
belly and it roared its mouth, and as it did so the
body spun once and a bright flash blinded them all
for half a minute. When they regained their sight,
before them stood a four-armed beast with a huge
ugly head. Without any of its previous injuries.

"A Serag!" cried Alexan. "Be ready!"

"You are responsible for what has been done," the beast said in a deeply disturbed growl staring at the foursome. "You have disturbed Kartuu and have incensed him!"

"No, no—" pleaded Khan before being interrupted.

"You have been responsible for my anger and...you try to kill me?" Kartuu said with a deep voice that resonated across the hill tops of the Green Bosom. Even the trees were afraid to speak.

"No—" Khan tried again.

"YES!" Kartuu roared. His lowest arm reached over and Khan could not avoid its large grasp. Alexan cast a spell that was first dispelled by Kartuu's other hand and simultaneously another was recast by the opposing hand that enveloped Alexan in a gooey clay. The live clay began to be absorbed by his skin and was turning his body to clay. He screamed in absolute terror, helpless to resolve his own death.

Kartuu pulled Khan up to his face. The snagged wind follower immediately remembered the time at Nivata Lake when his father had been captured by Krag in a similar position. Now, his new friend and only source of arvicity was being turned into a clay statue. Panic called. He did not listen.

"What is your name—entan?" growled Kartuu.

"...Khan..." he answered.

"Khan? Khan?" Kartuu was thinking, trying to drum up something that sounded familiar to him. Serag's were not just beasts but gifted with intelligence both in language and in thought and closely connected to all things on Seranor.

"Khan...Khan is the cause of trouble," the beast said finally.

"No, Khan isn't..." he tried to defend himself, not really knowing why.

"Shut! Yes!" The hand naturally closed tighter and Khan was feeling the weight of four walls coming together with him in the middle. Crushing time. He resisted. Alexan had been fully enveloped in clay and his movements had slowed. "Yes. Khan, bringer of trouble. Do you travel now to bring more trouble? I shall not let you travel any longer." The clawed hand closed tighter and Khan was losing consciousness. Then he saw his hair blowing in the breeze. A reminder. Nata had come. The wind, he thought quickly, call the wind.

Alexan stopped moving but the ring given to him by Ira was glowing. It was a brown ring engraved with special markings and designed to enhance arvic manipulation in several ways.

Griz had now fully recovered wearing armor caked in mud. His figure was imprinted in the ground. Once he was ready, he charged Kartuu's immense body with a primal yell. Inside the helm was a wide smile. The serag turned his attention and Khan took the moment just seconds before losing consciousness, he whirled his body into a windy form and escaped onto Kartuu's neck.

While Kartuu preoccupied himself with Griz's attack, Khan drew his batier once more and moved to strike the vital neck. To his surprise he saw Boon already half-way up Kartuu's back so he waited those few seconds so that they could strike together.

Kartuu moved on Griz but Griz had already arrived close enough to strike with his giant clavus. The clavus head crashed down hard on the extended hand from Kartuu and nearly severed the lower right one. His clavus lodged itself in Serag's wrist. He roared as if he had been bitten. At the same time, two strikes, on each side of his neck, hit deep.

Vital gouges that sapped the beast's vitality. Kartuu reeled around as Khan carried Boon to safety. Griz didn't stop. He grabbed his long batier and kept attacking. If not for his abnormal strength he would have had no chance but each strike punched deep enough to wound Kartuu whose milk now poured from several areas. The reddish milky wounds covered Griz who found it difficult to see after a while but hitting a large building needed no eyes and he swung as hard as he could.

The Serag choked and spit a thick red liquid until he could speak. "You cannot kill me! I cannot die!"

"I wouldn't be so sure of that," said Alexan, now breathing normal again. A whitish spell came from his hands, much higher in power than he alone could cast, and it struck Kartuu's arm sending the entire arm flying over a hill. He roared while another spell, of the same magnitude, came upon him this time ripping open his belly where Griz had already been digging. Kartuu fell over reeling and bleeding down the hill. As the heavy serag hit the ground all four of them also fell over from the violent shaking. Kartuu crashed hard down the slope. It stopped at the bottom only long enough to jump into the air and back into the ground.

"Mother farcking shat farcking Nivian slut!" yelled Boon.

"He's dying," said Alexan.

"He's dying? Father farcker. We almost died," said Boon. "Wait a minute! It's a Serag. I though those things can't die."

"No, he can't."

"Then what just happened?"

"We defeated him. He will die in his own way."

"Is anyone seriously hurt?" asked Khan. No one spoke up about any injuries. They had plenty of potions if there were any injuries. "We fight both for and against our planet."

Alexan had his eyes at the earth and his hand on his chest. He said: "Forgive us, Seranor."

Griz retrieved his clavus. "The next time, instead of running away, try running towards the enemy," he said looking at Boon.

"Hey, when two big ugly beasts want to fight its okay but it's not the way I fight," replied Boon.

"You fight like a luta."

"Listen Griz, you fight because you have no cerbus, I don't fight because I have one."

"Stop it. We are alive because we all fought. Each of us fights differently. This is our team strength if we can use it," said Khan.

"What team, Khan? We're just here for the zorn, remember?" said Boon.

"Gather your things, we move first then rest again."

"That wasn't so bad if it was the height of our trip."

"What if it that was the low point?" replied Alexan. Boon stared at him with that look you give to someone who should have kept his mouth closed. Alexan smiled back. He got the message. He wanted to make sure that Boon got his first.

"Crass armor always gets dirty," said Griz. He was more concerned about his armor caked with clay than anything else.

"Don't you have any feelings, Griz?" asked Boon.

"You mean for you?" replied Griz. That was enough to spark off the two of them and three minutes later Alexan was into the heated argument. Khan let them at. It would prevent them from getting bored and as long as no one fought, it was okay. Off to an interesting start, Khan thought.

He feared the chance of the four of them killing each other more than the chance of being taken by an enemy. This group was volatile and effective at the same time. He was beginning to understand Ira's strategy. Put together a volatile group to go against an equally dangerous obstacle. What were they in store for?

Chapter 16

BOTTOM OF the second week. Ira told Khan to cut
down communications to only when absolutely
necessary, that is, just highlight important events
like when they entered, when they achieved their
goals and when they got out. There had been a
security breach at the Terium. Information sharing
had become dangerous. Should Zorath or his
minions be aware of such a mission it would be
difficult to resist a counter-strike force. Ira was now
efforting that very reaction.

Khan and his party members had not only left
secretly but ill-prepared to face their icy enemies.
They were on a mission. Ira did not divulge more

than necessary. Unwarranted details would cause panic and could seriously damage any success rate for the tasks at hand. Under all circumstances, the Arvinstrum pieces had to be rescued or the fate of Seranor and its ceramin were in grave danger.

The four brothers-in-arms now reached an area familiar to the map they had been given. The last week of the trip had been uneventful. Only their unslakable need for unpredictability pulled them forward. They had reached the flatlands. Alexan withdrew Ira's hexagonal communication device and held it out to view the flamma map. The novice arvician and Aktavion in-training was an expert guide in the outdoors. His best friend Pala-del had taught him the ways to read the planet as if were one big picture filled with tiny images of messages that explained things and provided the necessary signs to do all that was desired. The map made travel that much easier.

"It's here," said the uninitiated mortal planetary protector.

"Finally. This last couple of weeks have been hard on my ass. I don't see the pleasure in doing this regularly," said Boon.

"Are you certain, Alexan?" asked Khan for confirmation.

"Yes." Alexan removed the crystallized ring from his pocket, placed it carefully on his left thumb and called a command. Bright colorful rays sprouted forth from the ring and spread out over the flat clay ground. The same ground that was marked on the map.

A minute passed. Nothing changed.

"Maybe, you have to do it again," said Boon.

"No."

"Well, it's not working."

"Wait."

"Are all thieves impatient?" said Griz.

"Khan, if he keeps insulting me I'm going to retaliate," Boon said.

"I'm waiting for that day," replied Griz.

"Get your cerbinds back to the mission or we will have to reconsider how we divide the wealth." That shut Boon right up. It was the only reason to convince him to come.

"It may take time," said Alexan. "I have initiated the spell but it is an ancient place. We should wait."

"Let's sit and rest. Stay on guard for anything. We don't know what to expect and we don't want to be surprised again," said Khan.

A half an hour later, the sound of large rocks grinding together sounded from underneath them. They could see a small patch of ground stirring. They moved closer. A ground portal, circular in shape, opened slowly. A loud exchange of gas, old mixing with fresh, came from it as if it hadn't been opened for a very long time.

"I love this Ira," said Boon. "I'll have to get me some more of his toys."

The portal lid opened fully and they entered a well-lit and beautifully designed stairwell made of what was one giant piece of a faded-blue ceramic. Khan walked in front with his batier drawn. Griz followed then came Alexan and finally Boon covered the rear. Alexan used the ring again to close the portal.

"Don't lose that," reminded Boon. Alexan just gave him a look that said, *I'm not as incompetent as you.*

Alexan would occasionally call out directions while holding the hexagonal device used earlier in his hand. It helped to pinpoint the locations of the two devices but was not so exact in its finding. Technology had developed on Seranor, thanks in large part to Technomicon, but House Levin was the main House pioneering new technologies used for infiltration, military and subterfuge activities. This was a newer model but at the time they left, Ira had already developed several fresh prototypes containing unseen technologies.

They reached a T-junction after the third hour. Griz grew restless though his armor looked new and undented. He hated being down here. Hated being unable to drink his anaprimo.

"Which way, Alexan?" asked Khan.

"It is not clear."

"Come on, we've been walking for hours," Boon complained. "Why don't we sit and have a drink for a few minutes while he figures it all out. I mean we just can't continuously work. They're not paying by the hour and there's no chance of overtime..."

"All right, sit. Just be quiet," said Khan finally. Boon sat.

"Lazy," said Griz.

"Farck you," Boon said.

A glimmering light appeared from one side. "Why don't you check it out, Griz? It might be something useful," said Boon. Khan and Alexan were busy discussing the location of the first Arvinstrum piece. Griz started walking over not because Boon said so but because he was going to smash his face in if he stayed around him any longer.

Five minutes elapsed. "Where's Griz?" asked Khan.

"He's gone wandering over there," said Boon.

"Wandering? What do you mean wandering? Did you have anything to do with it?"

"Hey, I didn't force him to do anything. No one can force that tree trunk to do anything," defended Boon.

"Anything can happen in here, Boon. We can't afford stupidity," Khan said. "Griz? Griz!" In the short distance, Khan saw an gauntleted hand raise up from the helmed figure then Griz turned waving to Khan that he was okay all the meanwhile walking backwards nonchalantly. And then Griz and gauntlet vanished and his voice, an effort to yell out, was drowned out by some strange mechanical grinding.

"Griz!" called Khan and started running forward. "He's in trouble."

"He's just farcking around," said Boon.

THE TRAP floor beneath the armored warrior opened and he fell three meters down, landing hard into a small cell, and more importantly, not breaking anything. Griz stood up, cursing wildly and analyzed the situation just as the ceiling shut.

Some other sounds came from the opposite sides of the two walls moments before they quickly closed in on him, two directions only, with large spikes. He moved but a spike ran him through completely in his right chest. He ground his jaw breathing forcefully from a caved in chest. The wall pulled back, he adjusted himself and the floor beneath him opened up. "Farck!" He gurgled and spit milk, falling another three meters down.

The second ceiling rolled into position and starting coming down onto his head. He reached up to stop it but even his great strength, hampered by the profusely milking hole in his chest, only slowed it down. His muscles bulged and hurt him through his armor. Without the girdle he would have been crushed like a ball of soft clay. The girdle's alien strength permeated every fiber of his body, activating his very molecules with atomic might.

All around this small square room there opened a wide slit from end to end. Mass projectiles, of only about a hand's length, burst from every direction. Some pierced his armor, some into porcelan, most bounced off. He got winded, his elbows buckled and he caught the massive ceiling with his upper back and shoulders, stopping it finally with the brisk potency from his legs. As the force of it strained him, ready to snap his skeleton, he wondered first about Number 51 then of his father and then of Khan.

The wind warrior arrived only ten steps ahead of Alexan. He reached a set of thick black bars that had come down to prevent anyone from entering the cordoned off corridor. He gulped down Ira's strength potion. His strength trebled just as he grabbed for the bars, extending his arms to pull the bars apart.

"Wait! Wait! Don't—" Alexan called out.

Khan grabbed tight and pulled firmly and as he did a massive amount of arvicity, kept in the gate's atomic structure, discharged into him. Khan held on through blistering blue flamma and widened the bars before being blown five meters back past Alexan, unconscious, burnt and perfectly still. Khan's light show got Boon's attention. He ran over.

Griz's face was filled with sweat, he was losing milk, but his strength, fed by his black girdle, and his reserve, did not falter.

"Khan," he muttered. "Anyone." He tried to yell but his sapped energy could not produce the sound he wanted.

"Griz, are you alive?" a voice called out. It was Alexan. "Griz, are you there? If you can speak, say something." Griz couldn't speak. If he did, it would mean that the ceiling would win.

"I cannot release the trap. Boon! Get over here, quick!"

"That's one farcking trap," said Boon, moving around to understand it better.

"This is your job, Boon," said Alexan. "Disarm it!" He walked over to see if Khan was still alive.

Boon took one quick look, inspected the wall, pulled out an odd looking tool and opened the trap floor. Now he could hear Griz's heavy breathing. The helmed warrior was almost to his knees.

"Is anybody there?" Boon said jokingly. Griz wanted to kill him right then and there but avoided the thought. Energy was very precious. Boon continued inspecting and fiddling with his odd tools. He opened the walls enough to see the hunched over warrior. Then he adjusted a mechanical device with his tools again and was surprised when the window slits once again burst out mass projectiles. Griz groaned as more projectiles hit him. A knee touched the ground. Then Griz got mad and in an explosion of pure adulterated strength, his absolute last, he thrust his legs and heaved his back up with all the might he could summon, the heavy ceiling groaned then cracked and finally collapsed as did the armored giant in a pool of ceramic chunks and milk.

"Oh, there you are," said Boon. "I found him!"

Khan came back to consciousness after a hefty healing potion. His hair stood in all directions and his hands were blued.

Alexan explained some of the details that Khan had missed. Khan was too tired to be angry. "Boon, you're on guard duty from now on. If anything like this happens again you will lose all of your pay and perhaps your life," said Khan.

"Hey, this is not my fault. Tell that to the big behemoth down there. Shat, he shouldn't go walking around like its his residence," he defended.

"That's why I'm letting this one go, but next time – no matter what – its your head."

"That's not fair. I haven't made any mistake—"

"You should be doing your job like everyone else every minute without needing to be reminded like a seedling," said Alexan. "That's called responsibility."

"Yes, Captain," he said cynically as he walked back to his resting spot. Griz came to and wasn't happy but he drank two potions and felt better than usual. It was the sight of the thief that riled him up and he could not resist. Boon was picked up in one hand and thrust to the wall.

"Let's make it very farcking clear, thief," Griz started. Boon had trouble breathing and felt himself about to merge with the wall he was being pressed against. A deep voice from behind a helm came at him. Some of the dents had been pulled out. Others remained. "If anything like that happens again, you had better pray that I die because when I come out I will rip the head off of your body and drink your milk while it is warm." He let Boon drop. Boon knew of Griz's reputation for murder. Message received loud and clear.

They all rested for a half an hour before picking up the pace again. By now, Alexan and Khan had a good idea where the first piece was hidden.

Four misplaced travelers walked down several more corridors and long stair cases. Down, down, down they went to the underground. Hours passed. They held a tighter formation, and with Boon's keener eye on traps, they avoided three different traps more deadly than the first. One had to be disarmed. Boon's talent shined during those tense minutes that held all of their lives on the edge. It also answered the lingering question in everyone's cerbind: why was this thief brought along?

Finally, they reached a small chamber with a substantial square block centrally placed. Ira's tard, still in Alexan's possession, identified that there was a strong presence here of the kind of the ancient arvic device they sought. The arvician dispelled the protective spells around the area before Boon went to work on disarming the machine-powered traps and locking mechanisms. The thief worked with amazing speed. He was talented, lazily so. The last mechanism, arvic and physical, required the cooperation between Alexan and Boon. The device was kept in the center of the square block. When Alexan analyzed that very block he, at first, found the material to be ceramic, but after checking with further spells it was identified as a *curium*, an element releasing condensed arvicity through the disintegration of its atoms.

Curium belonged to the earliest history of Seranor, a time when matter was more easily created. Alexan knew this from his father who had records of ancient details and prescriptions, and more than a thousand tios ago many things were created. Materials, spells, objects of destruction, weapons possessed and embedded with arvicity were made that could unbalance the greatest Nivian arvicerers or Kozotalian shifters. Some elements had to be created in order to embody potent spells. But he had never heard of the artificial curium to embody objects. It suddenly made sense to the Kozoty. Artificial elements would not be traceable:

by anyone. The previous owners of this device had
taken efforts to hide its whereabouts. In fact, the
curium block was much more of an impenetrable
shield than a deadly trap.

Within the artificial block was a smaller
compartment filled with a heavy, colorless inert gas
that surrounded the entire device. Probably the
dangerous part of the entire ordeal. Alexan worked
his spells digging for those capable to aid them in
their task. The first three spells reacted violently
with the curium and strengthened it further. It was
becoming impenetrable. Striking this material gave
it strength.

"What is wrong?" asked Khan. He had been
patiently waiting. Griz remained alert, ready for
action, as a permanent statue guards an important
entrance.

"It's the element. It's become more resilient. The
approach is not working," said Alexan.

Boon had sat quiet at first giving Alexan the floor
but he couldn't resist for the chance to open his
mouth: He suggested that Alexan try to recreate the
curium element, temporarily, into a softer material
so that he could work on releasing the protective gas.
But, he warned, Alexan had to be ready to dispose of
the gas once it was released. Alexan considered it
feasible, surprised that he hadn't first thought of
that. He manipulated a spell, the amulet and the
ring glowed slightly, and dug it into the artificially
created block over a smaller area of affect. No need
to change the whole thing. He focused and worked
his hands to reshape the atomic structure. As he did

so, Boon pulled out several of his tools including a suction device then reassembled them all together into a perfect tool for the job. An engineer disguised as a thief.

The artificially held atoms fought back and then some of them were attracted away from their positions and slowly the curium softened. Boon was ready to insert his device hoping that Alexan didn't release the atoms while his hands were inside. The thief reached the open compartment and, in one swift motion, squeezed out all of the gas. Alexan had already prepared and stored a spell to contain the inert gas and cast it out. An arvic bag opened and sucked the gas inside. Some of the gas slipped out and fell to the ground. Upon contact it exploded, stunning the lot of them. Boon's hands began to be crushed as the atoms returned to their place, and if not for Alexan's immaculate focus, he would have surely lost both forearms and forever his only talent. But Alexan regained his full composure, tweaking it just enough for Boon to retrieve the device and pluck it fully out.

Surprisingly enough, nothing was said and the two worked together harmoniously to open the portal that housed the device they sought.

The first device was cylindrical, about a half-meter long. The two ends were thicker than the center which seemed suitable for holding. Khan examined it closely. The material matched that of Seca, the one first found with Anativo who later became his true identity as Zorath and decimated his home, his family and his friends.

"What does this one do?" asked Boon, feeling happy to have him and his hands together again.

"I don't know and I don't care. These are the devices of death. I suggest that we do not tinker with them and only focus on our job," said Khan, wryly. "Give me the pack," he said to Alexan who handed him the special black pack suited for the device. "One more and we can go."

"I don't see any treasure here. Ira said there'd be treasure but I don't see anything," Boon complained.

"Actually, he never said there would be. He only said that if it was here then we could take it," said Alexan. "You shouldn't extrapolate too much."

"Of course, he said that because he knew that there wasn't any treasure in this stupid place," replied Boon.

Khan had already moved on and no one had followed. "Are you coming? Boon, you're up front, remember."

They continued and an hour later, after extensive effort, found the second piece buried in a second chamber inside a huge round ball made of *francium*, another artificial element, this time the resultant atoms from the smashing of lutium and curium. They, whomever they were, had gone to the extent of creating a different element to avoid the possibility of detecting any patterns. Boon and Alexan, now experienced with the first ancient chemical element, went to work without problem. Cooperation had its benefits when it could be achieved. This device had two end pieces like large bowls, big enough for a large hand to go inside, and they were connected by a short, but thick, chain of the same material as the first.

"That looks sexy," said Boon.

It was immediately put into the second sack, white in color, but had to first be pried from Boon's hands who was inspecting it closely. Arvic glyphs lined the edges and the weight of the object was much lighter than he suspected.

"Time to go," said Khan.

"We should rest," started Griz. "We have a long journey ahead of us and my back still hurts."

"Finally, he said something interesting," commented Boon.

Khan looked at Alexan who hid his weariness well. "We'll rest for two hours so do what you need to do," he said finally. He knew that any more time than that would increase the risk to a phenomenally high level. Even the two hours allotted could prove dangerous, but if he pushed them and they encountered trouble, then that may spell far greater trouble. He wandered halfway down a corridor to wind shift, an Equist's recuperative and meditative stance, while the others rested. Griz and Boon slept, backs to the wall.

Chapter 17

LESS THAN an hour and a half into his wind shift,
Khan became restless and went investigating the
nearby area. He walked to the end of the corridor,
the fact that they were probably six kilometers
under the surface excited him more than anything
else. Here was an opportunity to see things that
very few beings would ever be able to do. It livened
him. The corridor ended in a small antechamber,
not more than thirty square meters, that housed a
black portal in the ground. A round, black portal,
two meters in diameter, fitted with external locks
and deeply-set arvic runes lined around the rim was
set in the floor. At its center was a large green

crystal that reflected its image onto the walls providing a mesmerizing optical effect.

Khan put down the white pack containing the double-bowled chain to the side and moved in for a closer inspection. The runes were written in arvic code though were of a far more alien design than he had ever had a chance to study. He recognized several characters of the coded language. Each character used a complex principle stroke at the bottom that gave it a multitude of partial meanings, as if folds of information were compacted together, very much unlike the modern elos.

In one sense, he gathered that what lay beneath this portal was a gate outside planum Aquanomicus and that all those who passed would be given a vehicle to travel there. In another interpretation, he understood that it was the nexa hole, the gate of the dead. A third derived meaning told of history and evolution meeting together at a primal junction when all beings would collide and be forced to swim the consequences of their fate. The strongest theme that he could muster was that of an entrance for the creators, which he understood to be the Kozotal since it was they who first created Seragons which then spawned life, and that this entrance was one of four used to travel between planums safely, with a dating character setting it back more than 1,200 tios. It was not exact. The Kozotalians rarely were explicit and enjoyed leaving room for reinterpretation.

The last time that a Kozotal had direct contact with Aquanomicus, now known as Seranor, was when this gate was sealed by the green crystal. The

Kozotal, as far as he knew, had disconnected themselves from Seranor to protect the planet from the Nivian's rage. Where this portal led was anyone's guess but probably left open to the abyss between planums. And so thought Khan, how did Ira come upon this place let alone the key to opening the front portal and tracing the untraceable items, and what master plan had they now become pawns of? Marginally answerable; especially knowing Ira and the scours of his reach. Curious, Khan was. Better to find out more from here, he concluded.

Khan, curiosity fully engaged, moved closer, touching an unidentifiable character then caught his image in the multifaceted green crystal. A hundred reflections of himself were revealed in its shimmer, but it was the center image that moved his corius. It was the reflection of a seed, the seed called Shev'la. He was crying. Little Shev'la could not stop crying until his tears became milk. At that point, the white-eyed seed smiled then laughed and Khan, body and kol, was swallowed into the crystal without as so much as a whisper. The only physical trace that remained was the pack he had so carefully placed on the floor before he was invited as a guest.

Khan was missing for too long and Griz couldn't help but to notice even in his sleep so he went on a search. He found the unmistakable white pack then caught his own reflection in the crystal. Alexan happened to have been several steps behind the helmed warrior and when he rounded the corner, Griz was gone. "Boon, get up. Boon—" Alexan called as he himself approached the area. Boon woke up, and seeing no one around walked over to the sound where the footsteps last originated. When he then rounded the corner, he was just in time to see Alexan swallowed into the crystal from a photon ray connected to his eyes. The black pack dropped right beside the white one already there.

"Alexan, stop shatting around," he said to no answer. All was dead quiet. "Where did everyone go?" Still no answer. "Wake up, Boon. It's a dream," he said and slapped his own face. Nothing had changed. After ten minutes of searching around and finding none of his team members he began to worry. It was deathly silent. "I'm sorry about my behavior, c'mon, we have to get going."

He approached the black portal this time cautiously and slipped on the pair of dark glasses that Ira gave him to avoid the gaze of the crystal. If they were anywhere, I would bet it's in here, he said to himself taking pleasure in speaking to no one around. He was used to being alone in his profession but not realizing it, he had grown somewhat comfortable with his newfound friends. They challenged his intellect.

The smooth, warm wall not only provided his back support when he sat on the floor beside the two sacks but it gave his cerbind a sense of substantiality. One minute, three team members were around, and the next, there was no one except himself. How he wished that he was still dreaming or they were playing a long prank on him because of his selfishness. He'd been alone and closed off for so long that selfishness gave him the shield with which to protect his own sense of inner weakness. He even tried going back to sleep hoping that when he awoke they would be there again. They weren't.

THIEVING HAD always essentially been a process of self preservation and juggling trade imbalances. It had been taught to Boon, whose real name was Lafuratimus Boon – he had tried to forget it – that the self was to be protected against any feelings of deficiency or pain. Boon's family, two blank-faced overweight entans who left him inside an empty house as a joke and then, preoccupied with an interesting life, forgot about him altogether, removed themselves early in the game of his life. He was born different from the other seeds. Young Boon's body was tan in color and his hair of a natural green dye. No explanation was given to him about it. Other Seronians feared the little seed. But he was not without ability and adapted to the situation by distancing himself from all others and maintaining the position of a catalyst of things to happen.

His gaunt-faced early teacher, Yuntipo-lo, thought that Boon had potential as one who could balance trade exchanges, or as more commonly referred to as thieving, but thieving on Seranor had really come about as a way for exchanges to be more easily facilitated. Wealth imbalance was never an old problem. It was a new problem, ever since the advent of zorn and the monetary system. This had caused many more thieves to spring out from their holes to earn a sizable chunk of zorn.

Boon started working as a thief at the age of twelve tios, always in control, with a mouth fitted with a serpent's tongue, and usually cloaked to prevent determination. Dexterity, deftness, and above all subterfuge were his greatest strengths, but from the outset he was blessed in the opening of things, and only really lacked one characteristic – commitment. He experimented with disguises and body painting early on until he learned how to make his own mixes that would eventually remain on his body as if permanent. It was only then, after his sixty-first birthday, that he threw back the hood of his cloak and spoke open-faced with others.

Stuck in the antechamber with a mysterious portal and with two packs containing two of the most powerful devices of creation on Seranor, with others in the game desperately wanting them, posed a serious problem to his basal self. Maybe it was his fear of Zorath winning or maybe his deep appreciation for Khan accepting him despite what he had done to him before, which no one had allotted him. Not in his recollection had anybody given him anymore than he deserved but Khan had been different. Khan chose to accept one of the most hated entans into his group. Boon did not understand why, only understood that there was some deeper meaning to all of this. That there was more beneath a character than in front of it. A meaning which had been lost ever since his parents abandoned him.

Zorath would surely pay handsomely for these devices, assuming he could get them to an urba safely, which, he believed, he could. Then again, should Zorath really accomplish his goals then there might not be a planet afterwards. That was an odd idea. He wrestled with his own cerbind back and forth until a natural resolution came forth on its own fruition.

He, of course, attributed his staying to going against Zorath, and would swear to it if asked, and in some ways it was true but he knew the real reason was for Khan and what he had done for him. The smallest act that made the largest impact. The tools came out. He held them in his hand while admiring the craftsmanship of what he was up against. The antechamber, the elements and the green crystal.

There was always something voyeuristic about thieving. It involved getting into places without being seen or caught and, once there, doing whatever you wanted. Thieving was like having passionate sex with a luta without her knowing about it. And when she realized it, or when she returned to her place, she would become angry at the invasion of what was most private to her. Not everyone could do it. Not everyone could make such devious action. His best trait, and the one he constantly convinced himself with, was that he didn't care. It wasn't personal. It was economical.

Enough fantasizing. Time to work. His next task was to get his three argumentative friends out and then get home safely. A vacation was long overdue.

THE PORTAL, incorporating a nine-bolt locking system with two traps – one removing the hand and one to remove the first body part to pass through it – was a challenge even to him. It took him a hour to get through it and a whole bottle of anaprimo which he luckily brought along, secret to himself. His own blend.

More specific tools might have cut the time by sixty percent. It's almost impossible to always have the right tools in these kinds of excursions and is probably why he preferred urba-based scenarios. He was noted to be the fastest, not yet the best. Urba scenarios were far more predictable than these alien compounds full of incomprehensible technology. The bottom line for Boon was: how much was it worth? This one was only going to amount to a flat rate plus bonus. At least he was on company time.

Once the portal was open he looked inside a large circular chamber going down about ten meters with another much larger black disc at the bottom. A wide cellular-shaped wall face was on both sides but he couldn't see exactly what it was. Just below that were two sets of simplistically designed countertops fitted with long crystal switches, upright. Four areas had an invisible platform for standing which his glasses helped him to see. The chamber was automatically lit but without source. It was as if the material of the chamber itself gave off minute specs of flamma in every centimeter and, once the luminescence was combined, it provided ample lighting. And, most importantly, none of his three missing friends were in here. He checked back outside the front portal once. Nothing.

He approached the cellular pattern on the wall climbing slowly across on his taut rope, the portal was locked ajar with one of his tools for easy escape should something unexpected happen. The unexpected always happened.

Examination of the individual six-sided casings in the cellular structure revealed oddly-colored objects inside and with some characters at the bottom. He estimated that they were either date or content tags. As he examined each one, there were more than one hundred on this wall alone, he began to see a pattern. Each casing had mixed colors in the center of the object with consistent whitish colors on the top portion of the object. He swung over to the side to confirm his suspicion. The same pattern. It must be, he thought. They must be sealed in here, body and all. Trapped by a six-sided crystal casing. Three of the casings looked clearer than the others and he assumed it was his three friends inside. There was nowhere else to look so he moved to open those. After repeated attempts he found that he could move them by using a suction cup device, put together from his thieve's kit, to suck out the object as each casing was flush with the wall. It might have helped to have a powerful arvician right about now.

Once the casing was pulled out beyond a certain point the body was resent to the green crystal and then released in a short but loud exhalation sound. The trapped bodies, in no particular order, were released one-by-one in a pain staking effort. Each one took fifty-plus minutes to pull out and by the end of it all his fingers were extremely sore. His friends remained semi-conscious for another quarter of an hour.

Khan, feeling as if he had been turned inside out, walked over to one of the crystal panels situated along the side of the round room. He started to play around with a set of crystal switches.

"Should we be touching that?" questioned Alexan, still queasy from the experience.

"It might lead us somewhere or provide some clues..." Khan said, continuing his illogical experimentation.

Soon the black disc at the very bottom opened and a dark mist began to swirl inside. It swirled and swirled and, as it did, Alexan noticed that the arvicity in the room was rapidly filtered out. The portal at the top shut and the four of them all became curious to know what was happening and instead of trying to leave they stayed to watch.

Nothing came immediately. Lack of arvicity floated their bodies like avians in the sky without wings or direction. They floated around and soon started to play in the anti-arvic field. Khan again studied the panel. Alexan studied the chamber tracing the source of this anti-arvicity room and found the relationship in the crystal control panel. Khan, meanwhile, continued to move the crystals around not sure what he was doing but hoping that some reaction would reveal itself.

At the height of their playing, six alien beings – malkarites – materialized in the center of the chamber. They were tall, rock-faced with glass wings and clawed hands with only intent to eliminate those in the room once they discovered that it wasn't who they were expecting. A battle ensued. Without arvicity, the party had to rely on hand-to-hand combat and the use of their hand-held weapons. Their attacks wiped out two of them but did minimal damage to the others. The four of them were getting injured and would not last the entire fight. It wasn't until Khan clutched his armored brother's forearms, turned up the wind's force, and using Griz as a large weapon, flailed the remaining malkarites into rock powder and pieces of glass. They won by a margin. When it was over, milk floated in the air as did dead rock mist and pieces of glass. Some minor injuries were sustained. At about that time, two other beings, twice the size of an entan and as thick as the length of two outstretched arms put together, started to materialize in the black space beneath them. They were taking much longer to assume their full forms.

Khan knew that if such lower creatures had nearly wiped them out then the next couple of beings to walk through that black gate would be more than a match for the injured four. He yelled: "Exit! Exit!" No one could hear him in the anti-arvic environment. Speaking was useless so he waved his hands at the exit and they all understood.

Boon moved first to open the portal that he had previously opened. He worked fast, cautiously looking down at the new guests. In seconds, the portal was open once again. The others had climbed up to the opening.

Chapter 18

KHAN WAS the last to leave and noticed a foul stench
coming from the two materializing beings. He
looked back just as the portal was locked and could
see the resemblance of a ill-shapen creature. Fear
embodied him, swallowed him whole like an ocean to
a river, one feeding the other as hand feeds the
mouth. He had seen this before and the thought
quickly roamed in his head searching for a file of
memory with which to rest. Then it clicked in his
cerbind and all was made real: Zorath and the ice
malkar, Raskavron. The ones that took his normal
life away and cast him out onto a new path in life
that was corrupting his cerbal processes, degrading

them, shaping them, destroying the very entan he once thought he was. The beast that killed his brother was of the same kind. Their brothers or enemies, he did not care which except to know that their power was far beyond the four of them could defend against.

He knew then that the mission had been too simple. No, he had been too simpleminded about such things. He became excited. Ravaged by the pain of yesterday and the possibilities of the next few minutes. An excited fear fed the fearless Khan.

"That should keep them for a while," said Boon, confident that they were safe.

"I wouldn't be so sure of that idea," said Khan. "We must go. They are malkar."

"What are malkar?" asked Alexan quickly, having already strapped on the pack and moving down the corridor.

"Elemental beings," Khan said while running forward. "They are far too strong for us."

"Malkar!" yelled Alexan. "What are malkar doing here?"

"Let's not discuss it. Let's get the farck out of here!"

The four ran up the stairs, black and white packs and all. Alexan carried the black one, Khan carried the white. Griz refused to change his armor into the light suit that it was designed for and fell behind. Khan slowed down not to lose him.

The two trapped malkars must have escaped because in a short period of time they had moved up the underground compound. One black, Frappizor,

and one white, Ramidum, malkar chased them.
Frappizor cast out his oversized arms and in front of
the party a thick black lutium wall blocked their
exit. Khan glanced at Alexan who already had his
hands on the Arvinstrum piece. The very double-
bowled one he carried.

He pulled it out, fitted his hands inside each large
cup and released its power just before the other
malkar cast his elemental spell. A huge wave of
aqua as high and as wide as the corridor blast out of
both gloved hands in a powerful force that knocked
Alexan back. He adjusted to the pressure and
poured it on hard. The malkars stood their ground
for more than ten seconds as tens of thousands of
liters of aqua attacked them until finally they flew
backwards down the stairs they had just come up.
The floors and walls were worn down from the aqua
blast. Two heavy bodies were thrashed and tossed
back from the room they came taking large chunks
of the walls and floors with them.

Alexan quickly removed the device, gave it to
Khan, and then worked on dispelling the thick wall
now preventing their escape. Ira's ring beamed
again and in several tense moments the wall pulsed
then vanished. They could hear the stomping of two
angry elemental beings from the abyss coming their
way.

The four of them ran up without looking back
until the last corridor when the malkar reached
them once again. Alexan anticipated this and
already had the rod out, sending out an invisible

barrier that the malkar could not break out of. They were not only ugly but angry.

Khan studied them closer while Alexan opened the topmost gate. The malkars were thick like tree trunks with glossy skin and clubbed hands and feet. Both Ramidum's and Frappizor's heads were shaped like small boulders of lutium, odd in shape and proportion. Their two eyes appeared where they wanted them to appear. Shifting here and there to see every direction. Even their strength could not break through a spell cast by a relic of the Kozotal.

"Bye-bye," said Boon.

Feeling safe, they exited. By the time Khan got outside he ran into armor. Griz had stopped without warning. "Hey, what's going..." he said.

Sint crusaders Kalia and Kalier, Nivaton Denar'ka and behind them a score of naquior zoldiers ready for battle lined the low-level hill. The emblazoned Ice Timor on their chests intimidating their prey. A low bellied laugh came from amongst them. It was the deformed entan whose laughter surged like a wild toy that couldn't stop because the button was broken. Finally, he calmed down and walked forward.

"Surrender the pieces!" yelled out Denar'ka, frank as could be. "You cannot win. These are friends Kalia-Sint and Kalier-Sint. I'm sure you have heard of them or their brothers and sisters."

Three of them looked at each other for an answer. Khan stared at the Sints. Time was short, that was a certainty. Kalia-Sint shifted her head. She sensed something, moved forward.

"Come here," she said. It was a demand. But to whom?

"They'll wipe our faces..." Boon started speaking as Griz pushed through to the front to give his opinion. "They'll wipe our faces into the land no matter we do," whispered Boon loud enough to only be heard among the party. Griz kept walking out.

"Griz, where are you going?" Khan pursued. His armored friend turned his head in recognition of someone there but did not recognize it as Khan. "Stop! They'll kill you." His friend was no longer in control of himself.

His helm shook side to side. He resisted, an unknown force, for a couple of seconds. "Leave!" Griz yelled out as a thick arm swung hard backwards. Khan absorbed the blow and jumped to the side.

"Griz!—Khan, where is he going?" asked Alexan, confused at what was going on. Khan shrugged his shoulders in bewilderment.

"Ah, there is a voice among you. You must be, Khan!" said Denar'ka, just as Griz arrived safely on the other side.

"He sold us out," said Boon. "That motherfarck!"

"Who are you?" said Khan, now halfway between both parties and slightly elevated by the hill in the middle.

"I am Denar'ka, servant of Zorath, the true King, and a Nivaton. You are master of the wind, are you not?"

"No. What have you done to him?"

"He is not my concern. But you are. Let wind and ice face each other once to prove again that ice is the strongest."

Khan looked at his friends. Their faces grave with concern with the thought of Khan fighting a malformed entan. Khan moved forward to match Denar'ka. Glances at Griz worried him. There wasn't a visible emotion much like the Sints themselves. Alexan held Septana in his hands as Boon moved into a better defensive position if the malkar happened to break free.

Ice and wind faced each other. The two spirits that could not be together.

"Who is your teacher?" asked Denar'ka.

"Equist Nao Li-Grum," answered Khan.

"Your teacher is dead," said Denar'ka. "and I am teacher to all Nivatons. Isn't it ironic that his denial has brought his disciple to me. I will avenge what he denied me for all those tios. You will pay for the squalid treatment he gave me."

"It is ironic that a Nivaton is Zorath's slave," said Khan, forgetting the situation he and his friends were in.

"We are all slaves. Is not Nao's student a slave?"

"Student are learners who follow a teacher."

"Nao was never a teacher. He was a wanderer. Lost in his own insanity and delusions. It is the weakness of wind to be ever changing. To make the sane by going insane. You are the weak who hide in your own psychosis."

"Slave to the ice and become confined. Ice is the wind's hardened defecation."

"You petty insults mean nothing to me. You are a piece of walking mud in my eyes. All that you believe in will soon die. Even your precious Ira cannot stop our ice king. Ora and ice will conquer our piddly planet."

"Whereas you are at the mercy of ora, controlled by your inner desires, I am unbounded and free to create," said Khan, not really sure what he meant. He tried to use the language of his master but the clarity and cohesiveness was not the same. Denar'ka would only be inspired by such verse.

"Nothing and no one can be free as long as they live in the Versos. Nao has lied to you and now he is dead."

"But I live in his memory."

"Then I will enjoy killing the product of the great Equist Nao."

KHAN BACKED up slowly not confident of this challenge, not matched to meet his challenger but it felt good to push his ego and to defend Nao who had saved his life more than once. The mission had been far more serious than all of them calculated and they were lucky to have made it this far. If he made it back alive he would surely complain to Ira. It was a big *if.* Denar'ka discarded his tunic revealing his rigid stance and stumpy feet. He felt his left ear.

Khan knew that there was no way out of this fight and that it might buy his friends some time for a solution. Griz was gone. He looked at Alexan and

Boon speaking with his eyes hoping that they'd understand that he was in trouble and that they had better find a way to escape. Then Khan turned back to Denar'ka with an increased sense of self, remembering some of what his teacher taught him. Nao's face flashed in his head.

"Wind in your eye!" screamed Khan. He whirled into his stance not wanting to let Denar'ka touch him. They stood and watched each other for what seemed like ten minutes. Denar'ka attacked first, fast and furious he came. Khan moved light and airy to dodge the first series of powerful attacks. He felt the cold on his skin but for some reason did not fear it or sense that it could hurt him. Again came the malformed entan and Khan whirled and spun to safety, this time breathing hard from his efforts.

"You have learned the basics, Khan. But what you have yet to learn – from what I see – is that you have yet to have found your true form. And now I will show you mine," said Denar'ka, criticizing his inferior opponent. He moved his limbs in a set pattern calling upon Niva and her powers. Her spirit came and soon his body converted to pure naqui glistening against the sky. First Khan, then his party members, stood in disbelief. Only his soles did not burn into the ground.

Alexan fought against himself to use Septana and it was Boon who stopped him.

"I do not know about the wind nor ice but I know that if you pull a luto from such a challenge he will, his whole life, hate those who interfered," whispered Boon convincingly to the arvician.

"Without form you will surely die!" said Denar'ka. "It is the weakness of those developing. The students are the most vulnerable." Khan raced through his training trying to find something to help him out of this situation. Thoughts passed through his head and he filtered what he could. Still nothing. Too late. Denar'ka attacked. Khan, getting more and more confused by his misdirected thoughts, let go of his cerbind and in an instant became pure wind surprising both him and his opponent. Denar'ka hit the ground and changed part of it to ice, turning in anger against his windy foe. The second ice attack braised Khan's shoulder and it froze, limiting its movement. He became angered and twisted into a small tornado around his opponent disorienting him while he landed safely away.

He caught Alexan's eyes. Alexan was readying for something but the Sints were too close. Khan shook his head.

Denar'ka came again catching Khan by the arms and by a natural desire to live Khan turned his whole body into a windy form still shaped as an entan. It shed off the naqui essence that was freezing his limbs and his milk. Denar'ka held. Khan screamed in pain as naqui essence passed through him. There was something familiar and friendly about the naqui flowing through him. It was enriching him. He fought to control the wind state and became more wind than entan. Denar'ka, in his desire to win against his weak opponent, did not realize that his own energy was being siphoned off into the air and when weakened, let Khan go. He whooshed near to his friends, then reformed into his self, breathing hard but feeling slightly vitalized. Denar'ka dropped to one knee, weakened by the loss of essence and returned to his normal form. His knee had burned a hole into the ground. He stood up and brushed off the dirt from his leg.

"You have ten seconds to surrender the items or we will take them from you," said Denar'ka, breathing heavier than normal. The two Sints unsheathed their raders and took two steps forward.

"Listen to me," Khan said in a weak voice just loud enough for his friend to hear. "Alexan, release the two malkar."

"What?"

"They can help us."

"Are you insane?" asked Alexan, knowing what the answer was already.

"Listen. Release them as you hand over the items then everyone run to your talins."

"What about Griz?"

"Something has happened to him. I will try to lure him away."

"Time is short!" said Denar'ka.

"Alexan, go!"

"What about you?"

"I can move when the time comes."

Alexan and Boon moved up slowly toward the approaching Kalia-Sint and Kalier-Sint. Alongside was Griz, serious and steady. Khan had started walking to the flank of them trying to get Griz's attention. Kalia-Sint gave a command to Griz and off he was.

"You are all above your heads! It is unfortunate," Denar'ka said from behind.

At several meters away, Alexan removed the item remembering to cancel the spell he just cast underground before dropping it in front. Boon followed suit. They walked slowly backwards in unison. Kalia-Sint picked them both up.

Griz held his clavus ready to strike his old friend. "Griz, it's me, Khan. Wake up, buddy. There's a spell on you…"

"We're going now," said Boon, still walking back. Griz and Khan had reached the talins when Denar'ka yelled, "Eliminate them! All of them!" Kalier-Sint and Kalia-Sint stepped to the side to allow the naqui zoldiers through. Griz charged.

At that exact moment, the entrance gate burst open from the force of two angry malkars. A bolt of flamma knocked Ramidum over and Frappizor automatically attacked the Sint who sent it. Powerful arvicity and elemental energies exploded everywhere. The three weary adventurers all ran to their talins. Griz stopped his charge, confused.

"Griz! This way. Come on!" said Khan to his friend. Denar'ka's glare read plain and simple: They would meet again. Khan promised with a raised fist. He and the rest of Zorath's minions were engulfed in a haze of arvicity and elemental energies.

The Sints and malkar battled, arvicity erupted in the area and in its luminescence the foursome escaped.

Chapter 19

THE AREA that Alexan chose for a resting spot was balanced by nature's elements on all sides: clay to their backs, cora on the left, a flowing creek to the right and the padding of native blue clouds above them. The four of them, worn and battered like gurgled aqua, spilled about the area in disarray. The clouds of discontent filled all of their faces.

"They will come after us," said Boon, worried about his safety and questioning the fact that he would still be alive to collect his salary.

"Calm yourself, Boon," said Alexan. "They have no further reason to chase us."

"How can you be sure?"

"Denar'ka has the two pieces to the Arvinstrum..."

"And we helped him get it."

"They had known about this...Ira's communications...I should have known more clearly..." said Khan. "Zorath will have the whole set soon enough." He looked over at Griz, stooped by a creek.

"There goes the bonus," added Boon. "If we make it back."

"What happened?" Khan asked plainly, referring to Griz's actions at the encounter.

No response.

The lug sat harmlessly by a narrow creek singing an aquatic tune as it flowed gently through the tall clay embankment, carrying away the frustrations in the air.

"Griz, do you know what you did?" Khan asked, again.

"No," he replied.

"You were ready to kill me."

Once again Griz did not answer; instead, he cupped his hands, scooped them full of aqua and threw it over his helmless face to wash away the guilt, but the bad feelings would not wash away so easily. He had betrayed Khan, his party and himself. And he was unable to stop such action. He could only remember the beginning and the end and that was too much for him to bear. Griz's thoughts surrendered to the subsequent splash of cool aqua. Sweat from 51, his beautiful Number 51, cloaked his frailties. He relished in her imaginary silkiness.

A soothing breeze brought back Khan to his senses, away from the drudgery they had just witnessed. Away from the Arvinstrum and to the mistakes that were made. Griz remained quietly beside him washing his face in the creek.

"Ira is not going to pay," Boon started. "We came here for nothing but to be sacrificial morb. There was no chance in the Versos that we could have escaped alive and intact. Two Sints!—Damn Ira! And some ice mudhead. He knew it would turn out like this. Now he is not going to pay anything because we have nothing. Nothing! Our pockets are empty. And what was that all about just now, helmhead?" He turned to Griz. "You turned on us in the middle of a fight. You sold us out, didn't you?"

"He didn't sell us out," said Khan.

Boon, arms hastily crossed in unfriendly disposition, faced Khan. "How do you know? This serag-sized armor ball went to the other side and they didn't even touch him. How can you say that he didn't sell us out?—He did." The thief turned to helmless warrior. "Hey Griz, why did you sell us out?"

"Don't push yourself too far," warned Khan. A trio of young morb once accused Griz of looking too long in the direction of their table. He had walked slowly up to them with his clavus and busted all three of them down into irregular chunks of clay meat. That was only after the first glass of anaprimo.

Boon wouldn't listen. "We should've left you back there because that is where you belong with the enemy, I mean…"

Griz stood up, walked over and picked up Boon in one hand while he was still talking and threw him into the creek, head first. Boon's high agility helped him to adjust his body in mid-air and, as usual, fell feet first. Khan was unable to dodge the resultant splash and got wet.

The heavily armored warrior did a one-eighty and the back of his wide breastplate faced Boon. "You saved my life so I spare yours. I did not sell out. Something happened, a spell, a force, something…they are the Sints and all are enchanted with great ability," he said slow and clear, even the violent have firsts for explaining events. The response was more likely for Khan than for the thief. "It wiped my cerbind and my resistance with one command." He grabbed his black girdle firmly with both hands. A cool feeling reverberated throughout his body. He was comforted by it and that caught Khan's attention. "Some other entity controlled me."

"Did you ever have that girdle identified, Griz?" Khan asked.

"No."

"Why not?"

"It is a simple device with a simple purpose."

"It might be a good idea to have it checked over. Who knows what—"

"No need."

Boon wiped the wet hair from his eyes. He should have known better than to accuse the unsociable bruiser. And should have known better than to continue his probing.

"What? Enlighten us. Things happen every minute. What happened back there?" said Boon, calm and with a need to have an answer.

"Something."

The thief, soaking wet, walked up to Griz to grab both his shoulders. Griz raised his arms together at the front of his chest and Boon's hands missed and fell onto his girdle by default. An automatic hand clutched Boon's throat while the other struck the body hard sending Boon back into the creek, this time in a motionless heap. Learning to control his mouth was a skill that Boon hadn't mastered yet.

"Why did you that?" Khan asked.

"No one touches me unless I say so. NO ONE!"

"Okay, but you don't need to hit the team—"

"*There is no* team."

"What's the matter with you, lately? You'd better take a walk before Boon wakes. I don't want anymore milkshed today."

Griz understood and left the area.

BOON AWOKE angry as ever but his hunger overtook him and a strong glare from Khan convinced him to eat. The girdle stayed in Khan's head. Ever since finding that girdle in Escarotian's tomb he had become different. Griz was very protective of the girdle to the point of death. He had become more violent since finding that girdle. The black chained piece was very unique and Khan recalled when Ira had explained about the Sint crusaders he made mention of the Qari – five energized items designed as a complete set and one of the pieces to the set was a girdle. Could Griz be wearing a Sint's girdle? How could it have gotten into the tomb? Which reminded him, where was Pyx?

Arvitized objects, richly embedded with dynamic arvicity, were appearing in larger numbers across the world. The first wave of pioneers who fought to maintain stability used many arvitized items; mainly weapons, armor and arvic enhancers to rid their enemy, especially during the first and second Cerborian Repulsion (CR 1 & CR 2). Items were charged with varying amounts of arvicity based on the type of object and the level of caster. High level arvicians who were capable of warping arvic rivers arvitized a number of powerful weapons to fight against the Nivators and the Malkar. Cerbors and morb were washed clean from the land in groups of hundreds and even thousands when facing such relics. The greater the enchantment, the greater the translucency of an item. Exceptions were known to be made such as the Ice Armor which was made an opaque crystal green. Weapons were also disguised to hide their arvic abilities in case a corrupt user managed to wield one against the entan forces. Colors were changed, sizes contained and abilities were hidden just so that balance was maintained across both fronts.

Materials came from Seranor herself mostly which she freely gave to her seedlings while the followers of ora stole from her and even took precious matter from deep inside. The material used to make Pyx was even more unique since it was created from outside of the planet, probably from planum Mettadi-di Flamma.

And the presence of a growing number of items such as the girdle which his brother wore so proudly gave Khan a reason to be concerned. If indeed that was a Sint girdle he wore they were all in danger. The Qari was synthetically manufactured by Zorath himself and none could be sure what lay hidden in its atomic fibers. The very same ones that granted Griz super strength and a deteriorating disposition. For now, there was not much to do except to find a way to return to Casus, alive and intact. Ira would be able to help in the matter of the chain girdle.

THEY SLEPT peacefully, taking the watch in turns. Alexan, who had been calm throughout, slept in a dream-filled world. Voices entered his head saying the most disjointed things. He tried to listen. To remember. Everything was so disjointed. There were voices which spoke: "Seranor is dying...the Aquan sphere...seeds of Seranor...joining then be joined...you are the past of regret...Seranor will die, Seranor will die...we are the healer...the destroyer...sublime..." When his turn came to take watch he was more than happy to give the next watcher – Boon, who didn't seem to be bothered by it – extra sleep time. The voices ceased chasing when he was awake.

Boon slept near the clay embankment. Griz near the creek. Khan had moved away into a small clearing and was meditating in wind stance. Alexan could see his clothes flowing this way and that as the breezes dictated.

Morning consisted of some angry stares without action or verbosity. Khan's face, on the other hand, radiated health.

"We are alive now because of our cooperation," said Khan, as they chomped on some fresh chunks of clay. "I know that we have our differences – like any party would – but we should appreciate what we have survived. Not many can claim to have outwitted two Sints and two malkars. But we can. This will obviously make enemies with Zorath and, on the positive side, he now has all the Arvinstrum relics and may not care about us as a threat. Who are we to threaten him?"

"And you forgot to add that we are broke – zornless," added Boon.

"True. But give me a choice of being zornless or lifeless and the choice for me is obvious. We were lucky. My father always spoke of luck as a reason for something else."

"Luck is an anomaly," Alexan interjected.

"We are lucky to still have our salaries. And you never know. Wealth may come soon enough," Khan continued.

"It's waiting just around the next corner just like that ice thing that you fought," said Boon.

"It's possible, Boon," Khan said. "Why don't we just take one thing at a time. The ice I do not fear. There are worse things."

"Like being broke after almost dying. I think that's pretty bad."

"No. Like how to explain this to Ira."

"That's easy," started the thief and went on. "Just tell him that we managed to remove both ancient relics and, at the same time, released two malkars – as if we needed more on the planet – before handing over everything including our pride to the ice thing and his two Sints. If anyone has a better idea, I'm will to listen."

"Kozotians are not that absentminded to miss two moving objects, i.e., the Sints, that contain a massive amount of arvicity as they traverse the landscape," said Alexan. He elaborated. "It's an impossibility. I am familiar with tracking technology. It's impossible to hide such obvious power. Zorath designed the Sints that way, I'm sure of it. He knows that they outmatch our most talented and wants to intimidate us. He enjoys putting fear into society before he destroys us."

"Let's not get out of hand here with philosophy," said Khan. "We just tell Ira the real reason—we had the relics but were unmatched by Zorath's interception. We succeeded where they could not. They succeeded where we couldn't."

"Zorath succeeded on both parts," Alexan added. "He has everything."

"It was a mistake from the start and Ira knew it," said Boon. "This is all so farcked up."

"Maybe Ira was testing us for something bigger," started Alexan. "Considering the lack of good teams, it is possible that he had another mission in his cerbind. I think he even knew that the relics would be taken. Ira is not so stupid as to have missed two Sints heading to the very spot we were heading, and he knew we didn't have the ability to beat them head on. He wanted to see something, to see us fail maybe."

"We were the stragglers who were good on the inside," said Boon.

"I agree. He knew that we could get the relics out and that may have been his ploy all along. Get the relics out so that they could be reclaimed in a more advantageous position." Alexan's emotion added to his growing excitement with his revelations. "We were not the be-all, end-all. There is strategy behind this. With the two relics in his hand, Zorath might relax just enough to oversee something and maybe that is what Ira wanted. He was setting him up!"

"This is just talk," said Khan. "None of us know why Ira planned it like this. There is surely something wrong. We were no match for our foes."

"Not yet," said Alexan.

"We could have all died," added Khan. "Have you thought of that?"

"That is the part that I do not grasp fully yet," said the arvician, calming down from his excited state.

"He must compensate us for the excursion and the higher risk unannounced to us," said Boon. "Or my participation is finished."

"Finally something useful from your mouth," said Griz.

"Let's not start," said Khan.

"I still haven't contacted him," Khan sighed. "Boon, you saved our lives and to that I am grateful. I misjudged you. I would have put my zorn on you leaving us at the most opportune moment."

"Consider it a favor."

"Your actions speak clearly and you are welcome here among us," said Khan. "And Alexan, the same goes for you. None of us could manipulate the relic's energy as you did. We are alive for it. I am sure I speak for the others in saying that I hope that you stay." The blackness of the girdle gleamed in his eyes. Griz was susceptible. "We must leave for Casus by the finish of the next hour. Get your things ready while I call Ira." Just then the tard device illuminated. It was Ira.

"Khan, our beam, there is a problem with it," said Ira. His image was fuzzy and inconsistent. He managed the first line with clarity before his voice was cut out entirely.

"Ira? Can you hear me okay?" said Khan. "Ira, can you hear me?"

"No. The beam...is...pol...wi...discolor... Ere r u?" The beam was breaking up.

"I don't know," he answered then turned to Alexan. "Where are we?"

"Near the Aqua Nefast, I think," said Alexan.

"Near the Aqua Nefast," said Khan, speaking to Ira's dissipating holograph.

"There's a discoloration, I—" Ira's image disappeared.

"Ira? Ira?" No answer. "Where have you taken us again?" He was asking Alexan who was rechecking his flight path in his head. Khan tried to reconnect several times without success. "There's no connection here. It's black."

"…It was a shortcut to the path we took to get here," said Alexan.

"Where is here?" asked Khan.

"That is an interesting question…and I have to find out where we are. Pass me the tard. I need to see the map." When Alexan opened the map on the tard it was a haze of colors. "What happened to it?"

"Nothing. What's wrong with it?" asked Khan.

"The map. It's gone. It's vanished," said Alexan.

"Alexan, we must get back and inform Ira."

"I realize that is what we must do and it will have to wait until I can make out where we are."

"This is ONE BIG verdict," added Boon. "Now, we're broke and lost."

Chapter 20

BOON'S LIVIDNESS was difficult to contain. It pressurized Alexan and the intensity of it all promulgated by the top of the forty-fourth minute. As was typical of the windy wanderer, he eased the tension by shifting their attention onto a radical idea. Khan lifted himself up into the empty air screaming at the wonders of the land in which they were lost and noted, in the short distance of 300 meters, a cropping of tall clayish mounds with flat tops as if a giant foot had stomped down onto each of them to level them off.

His unusual play was effective. The three of them followed, steady glares remained for the first minute or so, up and onto the dry land. Khan whisked himself in Nata's arms and she carried him to the nearest mound about 8 meters up from the ground. He had aroused the seedlike part of himself in all of his jollying around and continued his distraction, even to himself. The others arrived at the base of that first mound. The clay was roughly hewn and jagged but moist enough not to hurt. The smell was damp and sour.

"C'mon lutas! Isn't this great stuff!" yelled Khan, crazed and happy from above. "This is our playground." He leaped onto a mound about 2 meters taller than the one he first landed on.

"Hey Khan, shouldn't we be planning our return trip?" asked Alexan. A tremor in the earth shook and Khan's voice was no longer heard. The trio had to fight to keep their balance and dodged to avoid the large pieces of clay that fell down from the side of the super-sized mounds. "That is very odd."

"What is?" asked Boon.

"That tremor. I usually can sense them before they hit especially if we are this close."

"Maybe you are out of practice, Alexan. We didn't get here by choice, now did we?"

"Khan?" Alexan called out. "Stop playing and come down." Still nothing.

"Where is he now?" asked Griz.

"He was last dancing on the mound tops," replied Alexan.

"That luto is crazy. Let him dance for a while," said Boon. "He's been really clogged recently. I mean his cerbind has been really messed up over this ice entan thing or something. The first time I met him he was much more succinct."

"What are you talking about now, thief?" asked Griz.

"I'm talking about the fact that Windy up there is scaring me a little. I mean he was grabbed by that liquid ice thing and survived. That's what I'm talking about. It's frozen his cerbus or something," explained Boon.

A second before Griz was about to reply, Alexan intervened: "Is it possible that the two of you can just stop arguing for more than a couple of minutes because we're in the middle of – I'm not sure where – and we've just failed the mission, and now our unofficial party leader has whisked himself into some clay mound, and we still haven't made it back to civilization in one piece. So if it is possible to shut up – and I think that it is – then shut the farck up!" said Alexan. His expletive verse stunned Griz and Boon. "Good. Let's find Khan and get back on schedule. We've wasted precious time and effort. And I, for one, won't waste anymore!"

The three of them, under Alexan's command, split up and walked to each and every mound in hopes of finding their playful leader. The uninitiated Aktavion combined his outdoor skills with those of his Kozotian heritage to create a proactive search strategy. Territories were marked by an extended index finger and given to one of each of the three members. They were taught to read footprints in the clay to prevent any overlapping between them. Boon, because of his expert agility and nimbleness, was given the task of climbing any mounds that exhibited a high possibility of Khan's presence based on the environmental factors and intuition, another way of stroking the ego in the face of adversity. Hand signals were used to minimize vocal communications so as to limit any misunderstandings. Finally, time frames were set up and objectives had to be met.

It was certain that Khan had been misplaced and, as that was the case, he would need their help to find him. Precious minutes passed and not a whimper was found. The earth, which had remained quiet until then, spoke once again with far greater intensity than the first time. It slowed, ceased and then came again with even greater force. The mounds started crumbling and the ground beneath swallowed the three upright figures. They grouped around Alexan as he prepared a spherical shield spell to protect them. The clay ground softened and the three of them were sucked into the earth, tumbling downward into the dark moist matter in a tightly-packed arvic sphere.

THE LONG shaft that carried his combined bits seemed endless and abysmal. One minute he was standing 10 meters high with the fresh wind in his hair and the love of light in his eyes. The next, Khan was spinning down a corridor far under the land which he sorely missed now. He was deathly afraid of falling ever since fighting Krag on Nivata

Lake when he was very young. The fall seized his porcelan structure. It confused his bearings and stripped away at his wind skills. Khan bumped into the rough surface two or three times in an effort to gain his bearings. It had the opposite effect. Meters of blackness whipped by his head and then he felt the cold air hitting him in a large wave. Must be a cavern coming up, he thought. He wiped the sweat from his brow, closed his eyes and assumed the wind stance. The ground would be approaching soon. Seconds before he hit the floor he fluttered into a windfall, a basic move to slow the handful of centimeters before hitting the bottom. Of course, he was able to slow himself from a much higher fall because of his advanced skill.

The deep-yellow tinged rock cavern was huge. He estimated about 50 meters across. Calwin used to be better at numbers. It was unlit, amazingly, bright enough to support medium visibility in the short range. Poor visibility for long distances, more than 4 or 5 meters. But the result of the fall was the problem. It was a long freefall, he calculated a rate of about 10 meters per second over a period of 5-6, perhaps 7, minutes: 3,000 meters plus in all. Three kilometers underground. How would his friends ever find him? Yelling was futile.

He considered floating up on the wind's platform. Three kilometers was beyond his skill, and he thought of a way to use the sides of the tunnel to propel him in groups of extended leaps. Suddenly, as he imagined his way up he became frightened of the possibility of falling two or three kilometers down, again. The fear prevented him from analyzing it further. A few hundred meters, that would be reasonable. A few thousand was insane even for his character. Time for option number two. That was easy.

Only one tunnel dug into the wall and broke a lonely path into the rock. There wasn't any choice really. It was tunnel number one or tunnel number one as far as he was concerned. His food stores were running low. Less than one day's clay nutrition left and that had to get him back to Casus.

Before entering the tunnel he stopped at the entrance and looked back at the center of the cavern. What was an empty cavern doing so far underground? Emptiness behind him and loneliness in front, the decision was straightforward. It was the same motivation that resonated in his life. The propeller which drove him on and into some other construct, and all the compositions of matter that he touched along the way shaped and molded the concept of his self only to return to the theme of his life. Would it always be like this? He thought to himself. That hollow empty feeling vibrated inside of him. When will I be whole and complete? When will the path brighten so that I may surrender to its sweet songs and join the celebration, and let the joy digest me whole and take me away from the pain that I feel everyday. When?

Khan marched inside. Proud and alive.

The air inside the tunnel was damp and slightly burnt with no apparent heat to justify the scent. It was wide, approximately two meters, and tall by twice as much. There was a cool mist that floated along the floor and swooshed to all sides of his feet as he edged forward with caution. His batier was out in front. It had remained unbroken, thanks to Ira and his technological prowess. As Khan continued forward and the normal sounds of the outside were drowned in the underground silence, he retuned his hearing to the sounds of his new environment. And once that barrier between worlds was crossed, when one environment is transfused by another, he began to hear a faint song in the distance. A lovely song that caressed his cerbind and kept him awake from the exhaustion that should have set into his body after hours of walking. He could not make out the tune nor what was said. At that point he did not care. His batier had dropped its point down by his leg.

He felt sleepy from fatigue and would have fallen where he stood had it not been for a new sound like a bell that rings to wake one from their haze except this was no ordinary bell. It was a rock bell which was made of rings of heavy pounding. Footsteps on the floor ahead of him. Heavy, rocky footsteps, at least two pairs. They did manage to awaken him and his batier raised back into defensive position. He had to remind himself that he was three kilometers below ground and whatever creature was approaching wasn't going to be anything like your average entan brawler. There was no place to hide and stopping wasn't a good idea in the face of an enemy.

The rocky footsteps came closer and finally he saw what approached him. They were bipedal and tall, a half-meter more than he, and from his limited visibility he could see that they were made of the same stuff as were the walls. Rock beings. He was the uninvited guest.

The rock beings stopped several safe meters in front of him. They had the form of an entan, general shape anyway, but all of their parts were made up of hard rock. The only un-entan thing about them was that they didn't have a head. In its place were two flat rock plates sandwiched together with a yellowish gooey substance, an eye, in the middle. They had stopped; therefore, they were intelligent. Even rocks could think when properly motivated. One of them, the furthest one on the left, stepped up and started hitting its clubbed hands together. This produced a rhythmic sound that Khan actually found quite appealing. It energized him. Then the strangest thing happened. The rock being on the right stepped several paces forward and started moving its body to the sound from the first rock being. The movements became a dance, not an regular dance, a rock dance. Khan stood and watched in amazement. Here he was, three thousand meters away from rationality and he was watching a rock dance in a long corridor leading to nowhere. He couldn't resist any longer and burst out laughing, psychosis was setting in. The laughing continued as did the music and the last rock musician started dancing along too.

The more they played the more he laughed and the more they danced in front of him. He lost control. The tension, built up over the past two weeks, came out in bellows of giggles, chuckles and outright wide-mouthed laughing. A mountain of stress and pent up dissolution burst forth from his mouth and, at first, he did not notice it but after a while he began to see the pattern. As he laughed the rock musicians changed shape. And in their dance their once entan-like forms started to merge together into one cohesive form, and then it hit him, he couldn't stop laughing. The laughter, now he knew, was feeding the lonely rock musicians and transforming them from his pain. They were sucking his pain and dementia.

Khan tried to stop but he was already addicted. Bad thoughts were pulled out of him. It stimulated his psyche. It numbed his porcelan skin and soon the laughter was sending him into some kind of oblivion, the same kind that is induced by excessive amounts of anaprimo multiplied by three in terms of blissfulness. His will slipped further down into the black and the corner of his eye could see the three rock musicians were becoming one grandiose rock singer who by now had grown a head, squared and centered with an orangey goop.

He tried rolling away from the giant rock singer as it approached him. Its two large rocky arms swung hard together sounding what he knew was his death bell. The hollowness, Khan thought. He searched for the hollowness inside the oblivion of his cerbind. He could not find it. As he rolled drunkenly backwards down the tunnel of loneliness he recalled Denar'ka and when he found his image he held it tight. Because when he thought of Denar'ka he remembered the duel they had and how he turned his body hollow, and it was the hollow that he called now in his final moments of life.

"Denar'ka!" he screamed, hoping it that the fragments of anger would waken him from his stupor. "Denar'ka!"

The rock singer had reached him. It laughed as it swung up both arms, ready to crush the puny entan at its feet. Two rocky arms came crashing down and hit the floor. Khan had dodged to the side. It was a combination of him dodging and the rock singer's taunting. The arms came up again, missing him a second time. Each time the rocky hands hit the ground large chunks of rock exploded into tiny fragments in all directions. Many of them cut Khan's skin. It was the next strike that Khan couldn't manage to avoid and it glanced off of his left shoulder causing him great pain though in his state he couldn't feel anything. That was enough to help him to focus. "Wind in your eye," he said. It wasn't the effect he wanted. He breathed in deep as the rock singer prepared another blow, the death blow. "Wind in your eye! You will die!" The wind caught, his body shifted to hollow form and a terrible fury of wind swept the large rock being and twisted it into a manners of pieces. Khan landed and breathed a sigh of relief.

"I'm not a fan of rock music," he said to the remainder of the rock beast. He picked up one of the pieces to examine it. He could feel a pulse coming from with it. The rock was alive. And the rock beast was reorganizing itself and rebuilding itself piece by piece. That was enough for Khan and he ran down the tunnel. Soon after that the familiar footsteps chased him. Rocks, big and small, were flailed at him from behind. He zigzagged to avoid them but there were too many and he was getting hit and hurt badly. It slowed him down and allowed the rock being to catch up. A large rock smashed his lower left leg and he nearly tumbled to the ground if not for sheer will to keep upright and running. Up ahead he saw an opening, perhaps a dead end or maybe a way out. He stopped, shifted to wind form, and swept up the rock being once again this time spinning him about before he himself floated up ahead. It was a juncture. Three tunnel openings. He randomly chose one and hoped that the rock being didn't follow. He heard the stomping come closer and then it faded away into the background. He was safe, for now.

Chapter 21

KHAN CONTINUED forward slowly. The musical sound kept playing all around him but it was distinctly coming from one particular source up a distance ahead.

The clicks of time gathered in the damp tunnel barely lit by naturally reflective yellowed walls were adding up and there came a compelling urge to get out of this place. The intensity of the urge grew and faster he started running into the unknown. Soon he was barreling down the lonely tunnel as fast as he possibly could, sometimes screaming to remind him that he was still alive or still sane to some capacity though he did not know by how much.

He ran tirelessly, choosing to enter two different tunnels when junctures were reached but always heading for that one goal: reach the stage from which the sound is originating. Head for the music that so inspired him. In that fourth set of tunnels, in the midst of his sweaty excursion, Khan hit an open area filled with a round greenish pool, filling the entire width of the 10 meter chamber, a pause between songs in the tunnel of sound. And in the center of that gloomy pool of what looked like rotted milk was a female seedling, not much more than 25 tios, and she was playing with a black ball. Not an average, everyday black. This black was made from the absence of light rather than the presence of color. The way that it absorbed flamma gave it a residual black as if a large eyeball staring at its prey. The room would have been pitch black if not for the luminescent green pool that radiated an uncomfortable warmth into the cozy cavern. Almost as if the pool fed the black eyeball, not much bigger than her own small head, with which the seedling tossed around without care or concern.

"Do you want to play with me?" she asked, polite and gentle.

"Who are you, little seedling? And what are you doing here?" he asked.

"I am Tammian. Are you new here?"

"Y-yes."

"I have been feeling lonely lately."

"Why?"

"Because."

"Because why?"

"Because no one wants to play with me." She was pouting.

"You want to play a game?"

"No. I want someone to play with my ball."

"I am sorry, Tammian, but I must leave. I have things to do."

"What things? Do you not have time to play with me?"

"Not this time Tammian."

"But I want to play now." She was tossing the ball back and forth from hand to hand. Khan felt that the ball was surely staring at him. "Don't leave. Play with me." She begged with the sad droopy eyes and Khan dropped his guard.

"Okay, let's play," he said unable to stop himself.

"Great!" she said and looked directly at the black ball with a wide smile, and Khan noticed an oddity about her mouth. One corner of it was up and the other faced down. It made him think.

In the space of thought, he raised his right hand to throw his hair out of his face and felt the wetness on his head spread to his hand. He was soaked in sweat. He wiped the wetness from his face and began to see Tammian's twisted mouth grow wider. Tammian was not who she said she was and his intuition told him to leave this chamber as fast as possible.

"Tammian, I am tired. I cannot play today," he said.

"But I must play. I must!"

"Then play," Khan said, not sure how to prevent the danger he felt was imminent.

"Good. Then join me in the pool and play."

"I will watch first. I am not sure how to play."

"No! You play or I will not let you pass."

"I pass as I please, little seedling," Khan said, agitated at the youth's disrespect and forgetting once more where he was. The smile turned into a beast's growl.

"No!" she roared. "You will play first before you die." She threw him the black eye. He dodged and it bounced harmlessly off the wall and back into her hands. "You are talented. That is good."

"Enough, little luta! I will pass and you will not bother me," said Khan.

Tammian, growl and all, burst out at her seams and shape shifted into a fat, smelly ogre made of folds of semi-dry clay.

"You should have played ball," the deeply-voiced clay ogre began. "You would have died a pleasant death. Vorkz must assimilate you into my brother, Korkz." He held up the round black eye. Khan could see inside and it took on three dimensions. The insides pulled at him, sucking him into it. At the last possible moment he saw that Vorkz had thrown the ball at him, he ducked, let the ball bounce off of the wall and then struck it back at Vorkz hard, who caught it. The black eye, or Korkz, had grown by 200%. Vorkz threw his brother at him again. He dodged him, barely, and struck Korkz harder this time. Again, the ball grew in size.

Vorkz handled it playfully tossing the weird ball-brother from hand to hand. "You see, you would've have played anyway. I am the inevitable. It has been some time since a being has passed me but I was weaker before. I am stronger now with my brother in my hands."

"What do you want, Vorkz?"

"Your kol. Neither me brother nor me have eaten for three hundred tios. No one comes here anymore. We have no one to play with until you came. This is what happened to Korkz after I had to eat him. You have made us happy. You see how happy my brother is?" Vorkz whipped the larger black ball at Khan who managed to hit it one last time before pieces of his busted batier went splashing in the pool. "You cannot play without your stick. Korkz must eat you. He can be whole again."

"I am going to kill you and your brother if you don't stop!"

"You will feed him and make us happy," Vorkz said and ripped the large ball at Khan.

"Eat this!" Wind and body met hard. The reaction bolted Korkz around and sent him back to its owner by surprise. The hungry ball caught Vorkz right at his fat abdominal cavity and started sucking away at his brother. Khan could hear the screams of its prisoners as Korkz, Vortz's brother, sucked the ogre inside, all the meanwhile getting larger and larger until the ball filled half the room. Khan had already escaped to the other side safely still running down the tunnel, and in one final expansion, the ball burst and sent pieces of ceramic, mud, rock, and the green liquid in all directions.

He was disgusted at what he saw. The bits and pieces wreaked and made him feel nauseous. Khan

stumbled and had to rest on the wall to prevent him
from falling down. "What in ora is going on here?!"
he asked, head down in prayer, with no one around
to answer. "Leave me alone!" he yelled, suddenly
spinning left and right trying to find someone or
something to talk to and then settling upon the walls
and the floors and ceilings as his audience. "I'm
getting out of this place. Do you hear me? I will get
out of this farcking place! My friends will find me!
Can you hear me, Griz?! I'm over here! I am
HERE!" His wet tears left the ground beneath him
slippery and reflected yellow in his eyes. "What has
been done to me?" he asked the floor. "What-have-
you-done-to-me?!"

"It is done because you will not do it. You don't
have the will to do it!" the floor yelled back at him
from inside his head. "The weakness tugs at you
and you surrender to the fear of what is and will be."

"No! You have put me here because of my
mistakes, because of what my father has caused,"
Khan muttered, unintelligibly.

He started running again this time scraping his
bare forearms on the jagged wall and ripped into
milk. He ran down the tunnel yelling out the
madness that came from within. "They will find me!
They will find me! They will find me! I will be
saved! I will strike Zorath! Strike him hard! Death
to the Nivian! Death!...!" Red tears mixed with the
sweat. The laughing started once more and meshed
with the constant screaming in the realm of
psychotic persona. His voice trailed off into the

darkness up ahead as Khan raced forward into his own disintegrating dream.

ALEXAN AND crew remained intact after being ingested by the land. The protective arvic shield encasing the three of them hadn't expired as it should have. Spells were spun under time constraints and for a reason yet unannounced to the arvician his shield had kept them all alive. At first he thought it was a result of Ira's fine equipment but after carefully browsing his cerbind, scrutinizing details with the logic of a finely tuned mathematical processor, he deduced that it had neither to do with him nor with his Kozotian manager. It was another thing entirely which he decided to put to the side for the moment in order to get out of this situation. Alexan, Griz and the insatiable Boon were caught in-between the surface and the planet's core. How deep they were was difficult to gauge by normal means though Alexan was attempting that very feat as the other two suspended their disbelief for the time being.

The Kozoty assimilated the natural information quickly but it wasn't enough and relied upon his spells to trace the nearest opening. "We are deep underground," he said while manipulating the subterranean arvic flows. "About five kilometers deep." That was enough to trigger Boon and his verbal antics. A brief argument followed before it stopped abruptly. The shield spell was weakening and it wasn't possible for Alexan to recast it under the immense pressure of the clay and rock around them. They were being squeezed and once the shield fell they would certainly die. Alexan also touched upon a smaller opening some 200 meters to one side. His hands danced together as the earth and rock and clay disappeared forming a small tunnel just big enough to get Griz's wide body through.

"On my count jump into the tunnel!," he said to the others as he continued to push into Seranor's flesh. The shield wouldn't hold any longer so Alexan was forced to make the count. He hadn't finished his digging. The shield collapsed and they simultaneously jumped into the tunnel one after the other. Griz was the first to scurry along on his knees followed by Boon then Alexan. As they pushed forward the ground vibrated violently and the earth churned itself and the very tunnel, their lifeline, started to cave in. They raced to the frantic end and Alexan removed the last few meters of rock to the opening. The entire tunnel snapped and was twisted together. Griz made it safely into the smallish cavern but Boon was half-caught inside and was tugged out by his super strong partner. Alexan was buried alive.

"Alexan! Alexan!" yelled Boon at the wall of rock.

"I slowed him down," said Griz, bowing his head low in remorse. "He should have let me go last." It was the second time that Griz, an entan that had never since his seedhood ever felt emotion, had failed the party. First Khan then Alexan. One by one they were being eaten alive. He wanted to simplify his life and the thought of killing himself passed over his brow. The thought was enough to anger him. Before, when he was alone, the feelings of remorse or contempt did not exist because he only cared about himself. Since befriending Khan and going on his crazy escapades Griz had grown a conscience and it was burdening him with unnecessary grief. "Farcking teams. Nothing but trouble!" he said. "Damn that Alexan. Farcking Kozoty. If they weren't so farcking inefficient and loaded with morbshat then maybe we wouldn't be in this mess anyway."

"Don't blame Alexan for getting caught inside. He's the one who saved our lives," Boon said.

"His plan to find Khan wasn't executed properly. If it was we wouldn't be down here now."

"Stop thinking with your helm and use your head. Alexan was good but not as good as me because if it was me – and I'm glad that it wasn't – then I would have done different," Boon bragged. He always found the opportunity to lift his own importance up.

"What would you have done?" said the voice behind him.

"That's easy. I would take—" His eyes brightened in conclusion – that was Alexan's voice. He wheeled around to see Alexan, dirt and all, standing there. "It is you!"

"I'm still waiting to hear what you would have done."

"You shat," said Boon. "You made it out and didn't say anything."

"I've been standing here listening to the two of you blabber incomprehensibly," said Alexan. "I didn't want to spoil the moment. It helps to have a good spell list on hand." At the moment of certain death he had flashed his body forward into the empty hole in the earth right behind his whimpering friends.

"Farcker," said Griz, straightening his helmet. "I'm beginning to hate spell users as well as thieves. Get me the farck out of here. The two of you make me want to vomit."

The cavern was big enough to hold six or seven regular entans and had a thin stream colored green running dripping down and into the floor. Alexan felt charged and noticed that his arvic stores were full. The arvicity in this area was condensed. It multiplied his normal power and Alexan relished in renewed invigoration. He experimented. Spells came with ease and did not drain as they would have on the surface. It was the dream potion for an arvician.

Arvicity flowed throughout the world. Some of the native energy was contained in pools, other flowed in rivers of arvicity known only to spell users while still rarer sources were found in nodes of concentrated arvicity, *arvispheres*, that compounded a spell user's power when inside. Black nodes also hid themselves around the land, moving occasionally so that none could ever wipe them out entirely. A black node, or a black arvic river for that fact, sapped all the abilities of an arvician and caused irreparable damage to those that tried to cast spells.

The arvisphere proved useful and enabled Alexan to further dig another 800 meters into the ground without problem. As he spent energy it was immediately recharged. The feat wouldn't have been possible under normal circumstances but that was much easier than digging 5,000 meters up, and was the best solution until they could figure out what happened to Khan. Alexan was unable to trace his arvic weight.

Once again they found themselves on an empty rock tunnel illuminated by a golden shimmer from top to bottom. It gave Alexan and Boon a yellowish sheen to their skin. Griz by then had become quiet and withdrawn. Alexan heard a sound, a musical pattern in the damp underground air, and decided that was the best place to go. If Khan had come so far, he reasoned, he would most certainly have investigated. Where there was music there was life.

About three hours into their downward sloping travel the rough tunnel changed into a perfectly horizontal, cream-colored corridor that had been carved by an expert engineer's precision. The four-minus-one looked at each other with the same question in all of their heads: Who built this corridor five thousand kilometers under the planet's surface? And why was it that up until now that they had had no breathing problem? Griz's response said it all; he adjusted his armor and swung his clavus to a frontal position, holding it tightly ready to kill. He moved on with the other two right behind him.

The sides of the corridor were engraved with colorized paintings that contained the images of

cerbors and morb with larger beings, blue beaked
and icy looking, commanding over them. It was a
story of domination against the frightful entans and
the translucent Kozoty. Alexan couldn't understand
all of the ancient verse but the images were enough
to convey the basic message; entans and kozotians
were defeated, and the two large snakes in the
background were captured by their enemies. They
were tortured and made servants.

Elegantly painted images, drawn by steady
hands, led them on until they reached a large
rectangular portal six meters high and four wide.
The only familiar object lay at the base of the portal,
limp, perfectly preserved and motionless. Griz was
the first to touch Khan to see if he was alive. There
was no normal indication of life. He lay in a semi-
fetal position as if he had been placed there and yet
no signs showed themselves to make such a
hypothesis even possible. Alexan tried repeatedly to
wake him without any indication of success. They
accepted the verdict. Khan was dead.

Chapter 22

"HOW DID he...?" asked Griz, too choked from emotion to finish his question. A question that they all were wondering about.

Khan's body slept quietly without a mark on his nonmetallic mineral skin. The hue of the portal reflected on his cheeks and an empty batier scabbard spoke meaningless whispers in the owner's absence. Three dumbfounded mercenaries were growing a conscience and in their cerebration they itemized the endless possibilities that may have brought their friend and themselves here to this mysterious corridor.

Alexan's mathematical cerbind punched its numbers in careful analysis. The factors that he reamed through were not plausible alternatives and he returned to his unsatisfied self. He even checked for footprints on the sparkling ceramic floor. No external signs were present. Neither Khan's body nor the surroundings had ever been physically handled by anything.

"There is no indication of physical presence or injury though an internal attack is conceivable," said Alexan.

"Conceivable? He's dead and you talk of what is conceivable!" replied Griz. The plates of his armor scraped hard together and made a grinding sound. He walked back and forth to keep up with his racing corius.

"I am not familiar with death, Griz," said Alexan. Long pause. "I once wanted to be an Aktavion and now am a sub-level arvician. I cannot tell you how he died any more than you can tell."

"Maybe it was a spell that finished him. You can detect that. You're an arvician," Griz said. "Don't wait! Do it. Move your hands. Try! Do!"

"Yes, yes, I was distracted," Alexan replied and as soon as he raised his arms to ready a spell he dropped them back down.

"What is wrong, Alexan? Why do you stop before you start?"

"I am empty."

"What?"

"My stores have been depleted." He no longer had the ability to manipulate arvicity because there was no arvicity to manipulate. On top of that, his own arvic stores had been sucked dry. It must have

occurred over a period of time and was why he didn't
notice it. He figured that it happened during the
three-hour trek that came after he stopped casting
spells.

"A few hours ago you were throwing spells left
and center. Now, when we need it you are empty,"
interjected Boon.

"That is right," said Alexan.

"What is right?"

"I have lost my ability to spin arvicity. It is dead."

Griz knelt down to Khan, removing his own helm;
muttering some verse so that only Khan, if he were
alive, could hear. He remained in that position
without sound or movement. Alexan and Boon kept
silent for a time.

"What now, Alexan?" asked Boon.

"Why ask me?" Alexan said.

"Because you are the guide – so guide us out of
this place."

"I cannot be the guide anymore."

"What happened? What is wrong with you?!"

"I never liked being a protector of the land."

"A what?"

"A protector. An Aktavion…"

"You have been bragging about this Aktavion
stuff for the last two weeks," said Boon. "We need
you to get us out. That is your job. That is part of
the reason for your being here."

"I am the wrong guide, if that is the answer that
you must hear. I have been fooling myself with such
foolishness. My father was right. Poor Pala-del; she

accepted so much from me and I took more than I should have."

"Alexan, I appreciate this emotive stance that you have just found but get yourself together for a single minute. I don't want to make mention of the obvious but we are currently lost five-thousand-meters, or more, under the surface of this farcking planet. It is a miracle that we can survive at this depth but I don't want to consider the ramifications of that right now."

"Simple. Death."

"That is where we are heading."

"I know," said Alexan, dropping his behind to the floor, head stooped low and staring at Boon's nicely designed boots. Alexan's hope evaporated and the stench caused Boon's eyes to close. "It's a good place to die. It will be more honorable than if we were back in Casus and the entire adventuring community knew of our massive failure." He lay down on his back so that Boon could see his face and Alexan could stare at the ceiling.

"It's not a good place to die," said Boon, opening his eyes wide in frustration and disgust at the beaten Kozoty.

"Imagine what they would say at the Ice Scabbard," said the downtrodden arvic user. "Imagine what my father would say...in all my resistance and hatred for that Kozotian luto; in the end he was right. Sad that I found out here, isn't it? What do you do when at the end of your short life you realize that you have lied to yourself as I have?"

"You know what is wrong with the two of you?" Boon began. "It's the fact that you are too emotional. Look at me, I couldn't care much about anything really. That is the best way to live. Stop caring so much about your father or master or farcking lutafriend! Start caring about yourselves. Your self is the most important part of life," he said, clarifying the way that he had lived his life up to then. And in verbalizing his deep-seated selfishness he became uncomfortable with it and he might have analyzed it further if he hadn't caught the sight of Khan's peaceful seedlike face. He breathed long and slow to calm himself. "I am not happy about Khan's death. I hated him at first and then started to like the crazy idiot. That luto was crazy!" Boon paused to swallow to prevent getting too choked up over the still body. "But he's gone now…and…we are helpless to alter that fact. That crazy seed in the wind demoralized our lives. He—"

"He got me farther than I could have ever done on my own." Griz said without a sound from his armor. "That is what cannot be denied. Look where we are."

"All I'm saying is this: He's dead and we are going to be just like him unless we pull together and find a way out. That's why we are a team, isn't it? That's why Ira put this insane group together in the first place. Look at us. I haven't seen so many diametrically opposed team members since, well, since never. They don't make teams like this unless there's a very good reason—It's fate. We wouldn't be here otherwise."

"You are onto something, Boon," Alexan said, a richness filled his eyes and he wiped the red tears. "Maybe Seranor had a hand in this herself. She might be trying to tell us something by leading us here."

"That's dreamy, Alexan, even for you. If I couldn't see your face I would think that it was Khan talking," replied Boon.

"All right but perhaps we were joined together for a reason," said Alexan, raising his voice once more.

"The same reason for losing Khan?" countered Boon.

"No," said Alexan.

"But with Khan dead we are broken," added the thief.

"Wait one minute."

"Wait for what?" asked Boon, looking at Alexan.

"Why are you looking at me?" asked Alexan.

"Because you told me to wait."

"I didn't say anything."

"Wait one minute," said Khan. Three heads turn simultaneously upon the living corpse. "I'm not dead."

KHAN'S VOICE was weak and grew in pitch as he came to. Griz had opened his eyes and jumped back three large steps, surprised. The previously unconscious wind warrior sat up on both hands, one on each side. Khan felt clear and calm as if he had rested for a week at the best tavern and ate premium clay steaks until he was full.

"You're alive!" cried Griz, gasping for a breath.

"Yes. I think so," Khan replied as the armored warrior moved him and hugged him with both arms, holding him up high.

"But you were dead," said Alexan.

"I not sure what I was," Khan replied. "The last pieces of my memory are very weird. I could see myself escaping a green liquid that wanted to consume me. All of a sudden, as I was about to die, something plucked me from danger and whisked me away."

"Could you see what it was?" asked Alexan, hoping that it was Seranor.

"It was a glowing cloud that enveloped me. I care not to think more of it and am happy to be back," Khan was still getting used to his voice. "How did the three of you get here?"

"That's a long story," started Alexan and went on to explain how they had burrowed their way down highlighting his excellent use of arvicity along the way and the way he used his spells to disintegrate earth and clay. Of course, the density of the rocky areas were more challenging and he owed that to the abundance of the arvisphere.

They rested briefly as they pondered on an exit strategy. Going up would prove extremely difficult, especially now since Alexan's arvic abilities had been rendered useless. Khan couldn't let go of the fact that he had been put here in front of the large rectangular portal. Could what was behind the portal aid them in their quest to escape? From a logical standpoint it was likely since whatever created this complex would have needed a way of exiting that was far more efficient than burrowing up through five kilometers of rock or traversing the endless tunnels each time they wanted to get out.

"Unless, of course, the complex wasn't designed as a place to return to frequently," interjected Boon. As a well-trained thief he was very familiar with complexes of all manners and sizes and from his own deduction this complex was built backwards. The tunnels were long and puzzling. The front door was misplaced kilometers away from normality; and the bulk of the defense, assuming that the portal was a part of it, was here and not outside where it should have been. It wasn't designed to be found. "Normally," he said, "the front door is really at the front and not deep underground where it cannot be found. This place wasn't built to keep the enemy out. I would venture to say that it was built to hide something. And neither we nor anyone else was supposed to have found it. Not without great effort."

"We DID find it," said Griz, stating the obvious. Boon held a wry smile.

"I have read some of the walls," Khan began. "The elos is influenced by oratic practice. Together with the images of cerbors and Nivators, I am certain that this complex was constructed by cerbors, slaves to the Nivators long ago. It is as old or older than where we found the Arvinstrum pieces." He went on. "In fact, the elos reminds me of pictographs that I found in the snow-capped mountains north of

Ghon when my father used to take my brother, Calil, and I, for travel and learning. Deep in a range of mountains hidden by layers of mountains thick as folds of clay we found a cavern and inside were ancient pictographs similar to these.

"My father told me then that it was the writing of the first entans who wrote in artistic images; long before the elliptical language of Seranor ("elos") was developed. These here in this corridor are similar. They are similar because they were derived from those earliest entan drawings and then altered by the cerborian leaders who tried to copy the advanced knowledge of the first generation of beings on this planet. And from what I can tell from these pictographs is an ancient story."

"An ancient story. About what?" asked Alexan.

"It is the tale of the binding of the planet when Seragorn was fused inside to contain him and his anger," Khan said. "We must get behind this portal."

"Why are you so certain?"

"I was not certain a minute ago but the more I consider it the more reasonable it seems to me."

"Reasonable for what exactly?"

"It will help us to get out."

"How can you be certain of that?" inquired Boon.

"If there was an exit they would have left it – or an imprint of it – somewhere, most likely behind this portal," said Khan.

"Isn't there some indication here. A reminder of some sort?" asked Boon.

"I have not been able to find it anywhere. It was what I looked for first."

"There is no marking outside?" asked Alexan, adding to Khan's test of ancient knowledge. It was the one challenge that he actually enjoyed.

Shev'la Khan explained: "The earliest races kept details available so that others could learn and follow. Cerborians – and morb for that matter – were the organized beings, remember. The record would be written on the inside. It would be of no use to Seragorn since he is a Seragon and would not need such trivial devices. He is a creation gifted with creation."

"So the escape route is behind the entrance," repeated Boon. Even he found that idea unfathomable.

"Yes. Maybe," said Khan.

"Maybe?" repeated Alexan.

"I would say that they didn't even open this portal when they were finished and returned to their bases from behind these walls. What we see here, this portal, may have been a decorative piece and not the real protective boundary that they designed to bind a Seragon."

"It could have been built to keep things contained," said Boon.

"But he is intertwined in the whole of the planet. Seragorn is of a planetary size. No, it must be something more specific. Decoration would be too seedish. We are talking about knowledge derived directly from the instigators of this world," Khan continued. "It is anyone's guess what they did."

Alexan said: "If I had my spells I could examine its power more closely." He was referring to the large door in front of them.

"We must do without spells for now," said Khan.

"That is easy for you to say," added Alexan.

"The technology incorporated into this complex," Khan said, "is very advanced. Think of the Arvinstrum. That is the purest level of technology very much unlike the enicoys that infest our marketplaces. That is what we face."

"How do we get behind the wall?" asked Griz.

"Boon, any ideas?" Khan said; the party thief was already investigating its advanced mechanisms.

Chapter 23

THE INVISIBLE door hiding four meters at the end of
the corridor, compelled the thief, who had spotted
the anomaly, to probe further. Boon believed that a
connection existed between the two portals. That
was mostly derived from missing pieces of
engineering at the front entrance, and the fact that
the second door was not visible to the uninitiated.

Entrances included two vital mechanisms to
fasten and unfasten the door, and all of this was
contained in its central architecture. The
architecture was built by mathematically-inclined
engineers who were able to design and integrate
complicated chemical, mechanical and arvic devices
to prevent passage for those who were unauthorized.

Boon called them "traps" for short. They were the most fun.

In their case, the front portal was missing the control with which to unfasten the door. It was not there. And he also couldn't find any traps. This confirmed some of his and Khan's earlier suspicions as to the purpose of this opening. The control switch was detached and his theory was that it was put behind the invisible door.

He pursued his theory and spent more than forty-two minutes to open the hidden door. It was the technology that slowed him down. He cursed more than he normally did since he normally had any kind of door, even the most complex, opened within ten minutes, but the technological prowess of the ancient beings were made with precise mathematical theorems and built into simple designs.

That's what Boon was paid to do – get in and out fast so that no one noticed. And it frustrated him even more after spending an excessive amount of time in these tunnels. The fact that it lacked traps made it that much more boring.

Finally, the ancient mechanisms were moved around through an intricate combination of skill, luck, and intelligence, and the door opened. Behind it was a space of pure black that no light penetrated. He moved in cautiously after applying his shaded glasses. His eyesight improved and gave him limited vision, just enough to get the job done. The space turned into a small cubicle big enough for three or four of them. Along one side of the wall was some kind of super control panel and it begged his hands to do their stuff. A handful of carefully made clicks later, the front portal opened to a quiet applause.

Four armed mercenaries walked inside not sure what to expect but ready to expect it with all their vim and vigor. As they moved past the elongated foyer, through another smaller door and through an antechamber their need for violence was rendered obsolete. There were no live statues or creatures or beings to fight. They sheathed their weapons except for Griz who had to constantly carry his heavy hacking device.

They made it safely past another portal, larger and more ornate than the other two thanks to Boon. His opening skills improved as he became used to the engineering of the complex.

The third chamber was the largest, more than 100 meters in length, half of that in width, with a 20 meter ceiling. The walls and floors were ornately carved of singular pieces of ceramic what looked to be hardened lutium with an exceptional level of purity. It showed no signs of wear or discoloration. To their right led a passageway that finished into a square opening. At the end of the large chamber was an area cordoned off with lined, squared pillars that went from the floor to the ceiling. And in the midst of it all, scattered on the floor, were several entan and cerborian statues with a number of gleaming items on and around them including a large clavus.

Boon and Griz both headed towards the statues that littered the ground while Khan and Alexan entered the passageway.

Alexan definitely felt the strong arvic presence here and it was what drew him to the square opening. Khan had been unable to feel arvicity ever since his seedhood accident with Anativo at Nivata Lake, but he too was drawn. It could be argued that it was his curiosity though in truth he wasn't sure what it was; he, and no one else, heard the beautiful music in his head. The musical notes seduced him.

KHAN WAS the first to step onto the rounded platform that extended out and into the next chamber which was also perfectly round. The platform was spaced a meter from the walls on each side and at the front there was another passageway that ended in a closed door. Alexan stood beside him. They both examined the room. A pool of red aqua, thick like flowing mud, filled all the empty spaces but did not go above the level of the platform.

Alexan was the first to recognize the arvic glyphs in the floor at the very end of the platform, but it was Khan who understood it to be a riddle. He had had some experience with this from the travels in Escarotian's Tomb and the two worked together to solve it. This time there were no spells or devices to assist them.

Their first attempt to solve the riddle went sour. The red liquid rose in height as a impenetrable and clear door came down to lock them in. The others outside were not even aware of anything wrong.

There was no sound or image with which to be curious and they went on undisturbed.

The red mud rose and filled the room climbing quickly. They didn't panic and tried to undo what they had done. They could feel the liquid altering something inside their very structure. It was reshaping their bodily material and they knew that they would not last long. Khan read the riddle backwards and, after solving it, the red liquid returned to a safe place below the platform. They looked down into the endless liquid. The door looked at them. Waited for them. The music rang out in Khan's head. They also couldn't get out even if they wanted to, which they didn't.

A second try failed and the liquid came again this time faster and more caustic in nature. It burned inside. It excited their atomic structure. Failing again might prove deadly.

Alexan and Khan focused, weighed the answers and then after several minutes of intense, cooperative concentration they came to a simplified conclusion that had to do with a cerborian military ritual. After announcing the answer, the previously round platform extended itself to fill the entire room. They walked up to the unlocked door and entered inside.

BOON BECAME excited at the wealth that was on the floor. He did not pay a lot of attention to the statues themselves since they posed no danger. The statues

were large. The three entan statues were made of
see-through porcelan that reminded Griz of the
being he saw on Inist island a few tios ago. They
wore an intricate loincloth to cover their groins and
had several pieces of jewelry on them. One of them,
a female, had a half-corset to cover her shapely
breasts. One of the entans held onto a batier with
only half the rod, sharply made into an awkward
blade, attached. The other half was found some
distance away from him. A double clavus, two-
handed and Griz's size, lay by itself on the floor. It
was simple in design and also had a sharpened edge
on the hitting side. Griz felt the weight of it when he
picked it up. It felt good in his hands.

As Griz scavenged the weapons, it was Boon who
plucked the few pieces of jewelry from the lying
statues. The cerborians carried their own weapons
which neither of them had any interest in. Despite
the lack of zorn, a modern creation, Boon was
impressed by the number of thumb-sized crystals
that he found and pocketed. More than enough to
compensate them for their travails.

"This makes this whole freak adventure
worthwhile," said Boon, wearing a sparkle in his
eyes from the reflection of the handful of crystals in
his hands.

The early generation of beings on the planet
turned to statues upon an improper death. Final
death was noted when the kol returned to the
nilospace ready for recycling. As it was the case
during arvic battles, in some cases the kols of beings
were not allowed or able to return for a longer period

of time. This process led to the formation of statues from the reaction of a slowly escaping kol within a dead body. As generations progressed that ability to become a statue diminished even if the conditions presented themselves. Entans and cerbors lost the ability to become statues except for those born of the first generation that hadn't died yet. There were some like this but they hid their secrets well. Even though diminished in ability, some retained the choice to become a statue, if earned over the course of their life.

The five cerbors and three entans here must have been involved in a battle. If a Nivator had been present they would be unable to tell since Nivators were not from this planet and their bodies followed peculiar laws that neither Griz nor Boon could guess at. The oddest part was the half-body protruding itself from the pillars. The legs and lower torso of a cerbor remained while the upper part had disappeared. And together with the half-body was half of an object, a square box with some evaporated liquid that was once inside and had now long been gone.

ALEXAN AND Khan stepped through the door and into what was probably the last obvious room, twice the size of the room with the pillars. It was funnel-shaped with the widest end at the farthest side. A metallic podium with tall and slender crystal fitted at the top was situated at the center.

What Alexan could not keep his eyes off of was kept at the farthest end of the chamber. There was an opening, a gigantic opening and in its center was an immense multicolored, scaled body part.

"Seragorn is real," Khan muttered in astonishment loud enough for Alexan to hear and agree. He estimated that this part of his body was at least a kilometer in diameter and filled the vastness of the chasm deep underground. He could only begin to imagine which body part and was stuck on the sheer size of the fabled seragon.

"What have they done to him?" Alexan asked.

"He is bound. Kept against his will. The stories were true," Khan said.

"This the source of my failure to cast spells. The arvicity here. It is subdued, it is..." Alexan was sensing something. "...the arvicity does not flow as it should and, instead gets sucked out. I am sure that this is an artificial black node."

"What is that mean?"

"Black nodes are the areas in the arvic pool that is devoid of arvicity. It sucks arvic energy rather than nourishes it. Black nodes are diseased areas but what we have here is essentially a black node. The only difference is that it is artificial."

"Another cerborian construct," added Khan.

The two of them examined the room further. Alexan focused on Seragorn while Khan checked over the podium.

The arvistatic device, a device that emitted a stationary arvic field such as this artificially created black node, that prevented Seragorn's movement worked against the seragon's natural rhythm by usurping his arvic energy and siphoning it off into some distant area so that the planetary serpent could not close its arvic pathways and was locked in place. The central part of Seragorn's body part was discolored, many of the scales were gray, but the outer areas were rich with color and were vibrant.

It was believed by many that in Seragorn's binding the planet was saved from destruction because the serpent seized moving and, thereby, could not rip apart the planet. Sagmal and others firmly supported the idea that Seragorn was incapable of destroying the planet which he was born to protect and should be made free in order to live out the purpose of his creation. Khan believed in the latter. Alexan had no comment to make on things outside of his understanding. The arvician knew of arvicity and not of cosmic deeds.

Khan stood on the podium. It had room just enough for one. There was nothing to read so he played around with the crystals hoping to learn something new. The music still sounded in his head and it encouraged him to play and play he did. He touched several of the long crystal shards. An outsider would have sworn that Khan knew what he was doing. He labeled it as "play". It was only when Alexan felt a shift in the arvistatic device that he turned to Khan. Alexan had been mesmerized by the totality of Seragorn and his cryptic history. The device which bound the cosmic snake began to lose its degree of intensity and was decreasing in size.

Arvicity started to roam, in tiny amounts, once again, all thanks to Khan's playful experiments.

"Khan, what have you done?" asked Alexan, a terrible worry on his face. Kozoty are not designed to worry.

"I'm just playing around," Khan replied. "No harm in that. Isn't this amazing." Khan was too relaxed and too happy to be in a normal mood. It added to Alexan's worry.

"Khan, can you please come down from there. I think you are effecting the machine. It's not doing anything good. Look, I think its hurting our cosmic friend."

"It's designed to do that."

"We didn't come here to tinker with this cosmic stuff now get off of it." By then it was too late. Khan had already begun a process, though he didn't know what, of closing down the arvistatic device and all of its effects on the trapped Seragon.

"He deserves to be free." Alexan stepped up to him and slapped him twice across both cheeks.

"What's the matter with you?" he said. "Why are you hitting me?"

"Do you realize what you have just done? Do you?"

"What did I do?"

"You shut off the device that bound Seragorn's body part."

"How did I do that?"

"By playing around with this control panel. I think that it controls it."

"But I only touched it a couple of times," Khan said. He had no recollection of what Alexan was saying.

"That's great!" Alexan said in frustration. "You shut it off." The arvicity began to flow more regularly as the minutes slipped past. The gray scales remained gray though.

"Let's go, Alexan," said Khan. "This is not going to help us get out."

"Promise me one thing," said Alexan. "Promise me that you'll stop playing around with control panels in the future. Will you at least consider that for me?"

"I'll consider it. I still don't know why you are so upset."

"I'm not upset. Why am I upset?"

"I don't know."

Alexan refused to continue an endless conversation. Instead he went over to Seragorn's body. "He is magnificent, isn't he?" His hand went out and he touched the large scales. He was immediately latched on by both hands and was being shocked to death by massive arcs of arvicity. His body convulsed.

Khan tried to pull him off without immediate success. Alexan's skin was beginning to dry out and crack, milk poured from his ears as he choked in his own milk. Khan changed to wind form and sucked him off. Alexan collapsed on the floor unconscious. "I really have to ask Ira for some anti-unconscious potions," Khan said to himself after checking to see if Alexan was still alive. He was, but just barely.

KHAN CARRIED Alexan to the first large chamber
where Griz was practicing with his new clavus and
Boon polishing his wealth. Alexan was adequately
fried and looked in poor shape.

"There you two are. Is he okay?" said Boon.

"Yeah, he'll live but we need to get him healed. I
gave him a potion to give him some strength. I
imagine that he will be out for a while," said Khan.
"Any exit strategies, yet?"

"No, not yet. But we're getting close."

"Polishing crystals won't get us out of here. Griz,
anything?"

"I have a new weapon," said Griz.

"I can always trust the two of you to achieve your
tasks."

Empty stares.

After putting Alexan down and assigning Griz to
carry him when the time came, Khan studied the
pillars knowing that what was behind the pillars
would get them out. The were seven pillars in all
and they formed a large alcove at the far wall. Many
inscriptions were on the pillars, nothing to help
them through except a confirmation that it was a
transport device. The pillars were spaced out wide
enough for two or three bodies to go in-between but
when they tried to pass they were prevented by an
invisible force. Alexan's arvic knowledge would have
come in handy then.

Boon guessed that the half-object that they had found had some connection with getting out. The only problem being that the device was in half and was empty of whatever filled it. There was no other solution and they had begun to feel sick inside the area probably from an overdose of arvicity that now emanated from Seragorn.

Khan put together that the device was once filled with the reddish liquid in the other room and it had some impact on travel. It originally altered their atomic structures and might have some kind of chemical reaction on the object's material to allow them to pass. It might just be a "passing device" to confirm that they were who they were. Without any other strategy and their growing sickness Khan filled the object with the red liquid and one by one they passed the pillars with only a small resistance as if passing through a wall of invisible aqua.

Once behind the pillars they found themselves standing on a black platform raised 10 centimeters off of the ground. Khan imagined an area in Casus which he was familiar with, namely his residence, and the four of them swooshed away.

www.ingramcontent.com/pod-product-compliance
Lightning Source LLC
Chambersburg PA
CBHW031938010726
47493CB00007B/1984